Collins Creek, Volume 1

Contemporary Currents and Historical Eddies

Ron Collins

SKYFOX
PUBLISHING

For Mom

Because I miss her, and because it includes her favorite story.

Contents

Foreword ... i

Introduction: Writing for Anthologies ... iii

The White Game ... 1

Us vs. Them ... 17

Prospecting ... 49

Day of the Party ... 65

The Ten Days of Newtonmas ... 73

The Year That Went into Extra Innings ... 97

Bobo ... 113

Hero #8 ... 133

Look Safe ... 149

The Spy Who Walked into the Cold ... 163

About Ron Collins ... 195

Other Work by Ron Collins ... 196

Acknowledgements ... 199

Foreword

What you hold in your hands is the first of three collections of stories that are a product of the several years I was associated with the *Fiction River* series—a long-running project that was the brainchild of Kristine Kathryn Rusch and Dean Wesley Smith, and that has included many, many fantastic editors and writers from around the globe. The core of the project stems from a workshop that was held each year (at least until the pandemic brought every such thing to a slamming halt), originating in Lincoln City, Oregon, then migrating to Las Vegas, Nevada.

With a little luck and a lot of vaccinations, perhaps that workshop will resume in 2022. Time will tell.

Regardless, though, I've been threatening to make these *Collins Creek* collections a reality for some time, and this seems like the right moment.

The stories in this first volume are all pieces of contemporary, real-world fiction.

Perhaps that seems odd to my regular readers, because as Kris Rusch has often noted in her introductions to my stories in *Fiction River*, I call myself a writer of speculative fiction. She then, however, inevitably goes on to say I should write more "like this one"—noting that what follows is a crime story, or a mystery, or a piece of historical fiction. *Fiction River* is a place where genres can mix and clash together to make wonderful music, and it turns out that when Kris edits, I write a lot of things that don't have speculative elements in them.

Hence this volume, which is chock full of this kind of story.

As such, I've asked Kris to give her own thoughts on it with an introduction. I'm quite honored that she's agreed to do so.

Fear not, though, Volume 2 will include all the good Skiffy/Fantasy-laced speculative fiction I've put into the *Fiction River* project.

Then will come Volume 3, which will hold all the stories that have passed through *Fiction River* to be published in places like *Analog*, *Galaxy's Edge*, and *Pulphouse*.

And I love them each enough to want to see them all together.

I hope you'll like them, too.

Ron Collins
Oro Valley, AZ

Introduction: Writing for Anthologies

Kristine Kathryn Rusch

Here's the key to writing for anthologies: You need to think differently from everyone else.

Anthology assignments come in various forms. Sometimes they're quite specific: We want zombie stories of no more than 5,000 words, set in a major city, during the 21st century. We prefer to read about zombies falling in love or zombies with families or zombies that have day jobs. Avoid cliches.

Sometimes the anthology assignments are very vague: We want romantic holiday stories between 3,000 and 10,000 words.

Sometimes they're a cross between the two: We want romantic holiday stories between 3,000 and 10,000 words. Unusual holidays preferred. No zombie stories!

Most people write something predictable and down the line. If I sent out the first description, I would get a dozen zombies in love stories, a handful of zombies with family stories (dull zombie with family stories) and a small group of zombies with day job stories. None of the writers who wrote those stories would avoid clichés.

But Ron Collins does.

Ron can write something unique for any type of anthology. I'm not sure how many anthologies I've invited him into. (In this collection, you'll find 10 such stories, including the award-nominated mystery "The White Game.") Ron always strives to write a story that no other writer will write.

In his quest to be different, he sometimes misses the anthology assignment. A companion volume to this one has those stories...because someone else published those stories. All of Ron's stories are excellent. Sometimes they just don't fit a narrowly constructed anthology.

All of the stories here fit, but all of the stories here are very different from the other stories in the volume or project. For example, "The Ten Days of Newtonmas" appears in the anthology *Winter Holidays*. It's a holiday I'd love to celebrate.

He and his daughter Brigid wrote one of my very favorite of all time stories, "The Year That Went into Extra Innings," before 2020, the world's collective year that went into metaphorical extra innings. The extra innings in this story, though, are actual extra innings: the final game of baseball's World Series looked like it would never end. I love this story, and think of it every October when the World Series begins.

Some stories are like that.

With Ron, more stories than not are like that.

The key to writing an anthology story is to write a story that only you (or you and your daughter) could write. No one else. No one else could have thought of a never-ending baseball game.

Ron writes a lot about baseball. His story "The White Game" features baseball with the right amount of clear-eyed vision and just a tiny bit of nostalgia. It's darn near close to perfect.

Lest you think that Ron just looks at an anthology invitation and then comes up with a brilliant story—okay, well, I suspect he does that more often than not—every now and then, though, he writes a story and it has the heart of another story inside of it. He did that with "The Spy Who Walked into the Cold," for *Fiction River: Spies.*

This story was written about the Fred Hampton murder before *Judas and the Black Messiah* hit the screens. Ron wrote a first draft for me, and I loved the idea of the story, but because of my Smokey Dalton series (which I write under the name Kris Nelscott), I knew that Ron had to do some more research to get the perspective and details right.

He did. And he wrote one of the best stories I've ever read from him. It closes this book.

When I say that Ron wrote one of the best stories I've ever read from him, that's exceptionally high praise. Because Ron's stories are often the best in any volume he's in—or any magazine he's in. Ron's voice, his use of language, and the way he goes after a story make him one of the best short story writers working today.

If only we could get him to write more stories.

I'm sure that will only be a matter of time.

To those of you who are new to these stories, I envy you the journey ahead. To those of you who, like me, have read them before, I know you'll love the reread.

Ron knows how to write for anthologies.

But more important than that, Ron knows how to write.

Full stop.

—Kristine Kathryn Rusch

"The White Game" first appeared in _Fiction River: Hidden in Crime_. It was among my first attempts at historical fiction. I admit I was nervous about it. For reasons that might become obvious as the story unfolds, I felt a deep need for the story to feel right. So, once I knew what I wanted to do, I spent days reading every newspaper from Birmingham printed in the springtime of 1963 that I could get my hands on, and watching every documentary and interview I could put my eyeballs on. Then, on the last day before the anthology deadline, I wrote it.

When it was done, I knew it said what I wanted to say.

Kris suggested I touch the ending a bit—a suggestion that was so bang-on that I knew what I was going to do the moment she said it. It all added up to a story that went on to make the shortlist for the Derringer Award for Best Short Crime Fiction of 2016.

The White Game

I told the police I needed access to the archives for a story I was doing for the paper, which wasn't completely a lie but also wasn't the whole truth. That's the way of all things, though, isn't it?

The microfiche machine shut off with a firm click.

I moved the row of paper cups that had held the endless stream of coffee that kept me going all night, and I reshuffled the last set of aperture cards. The little room was warm, now. It felt stale, smelled of the machine's bulb. Its silence was a thing itself, like a bottomless pit of nothing. When I had the cards in order, I pushed the seat back from the table, took off my glasses, and rubbed my eyes. The bridge of my nose stung. My head hurt from squinting too long, and my neck felt like it had been bent about a hundred directions at once.

I'm nearing seventy now. Too damned old to pull all-nighters.

It had been worth it, though.

I looked at my notes, and, in doing so, I thought back to the first time I met Tommy Daniels. It was a Thursday. I hadn't remembered that before, but that's what the calendar said, and I believe it.

The rest of it, though, I remember like it was stained on the back of my hand.

May 2nd:

I was fifteen, getting on toward sixteen—that age where baseball was still the most important thing on the planet, but where I was beginning to see that Bonnie Del Rae might well have her charms, too. My Cardinals were on their way to beating the Cubs 4-3 that day. They led the Giants by 2 games.

Rumors of the Negro problems had scattered themselves around while I was at school, but Negro issues never created much of a ripple to me. So there was talk, but otherwise the day wasn't much different from any other.

It was a cool day for May, probably didn't hit 80, but the sky was clear enough so I and the rest of the boys spent the afternoon waiting for the final bell before we could go to gather at the park up north like we always did. The one across Village creek from the railroad yards. It's a place that's made up all nice now, but back then it was mostly an open patch of land where a million games had worn a lopsided set of basepaths bare.

It had rained most of the week before but the last couple days were dry, which meant the dirt was hard and firm, and the grass was the kind that made for fast grounders and wicked hops. Being a school day, it was late enough when we all got there that we had time for only one game, or maybe two if the first was quick enough.

"Where's Cade?" I asked Bobby Downs as we tossed the ball to stretch our arms.

"Miss Whitlow kept him after the bell," Bobby replied.

I wiped my brow on the sleeve of my white t-shirt. "Shit," I said, and I admit the word made me feel bigger than my fifteen years. "So we got no one to play short?"

"Reckon not," Bobby said.

"I can play it," a voice called from under the elm tree alongside the field.

It was the Negro boy that'd had been coming around a bit the past few days. He was thin, with elbows that looked like they ought to swivel every which way. He was not too tall, not too short. His hair was trimmed close against his head. He wore a faded red shirt with a collar, and he wore a pair of worn-out work slacks—both of which were too big for him. His shoes were scuffed and brown. I guessed him about my age, no more than sixteen. He leaned his shoulder against an elm tree alongside the yard and smoked a cigarette that looked extra bright against the skin of his fingers.

"This is a white game," I said as if that was all that needed to be said. Which it was, really.

I turned to throw the ball.

Then I looked back over my shoulder, thinking maybe this was one of those Negro boys my daddy said would come out to cause problems like the ones that kept going into the stores and the lunch counters.

But the boy was still just standing there, smoking.

"I can hit a bit, too," he said when he saw me glance back.

"Let's play some ball!" Jerry Lyn Keys, a kid from the Catholic high school, called out from over on the other side of the field.

The guys came together, all eight of us.

"Anyone else coming?" Omer Cash asked. Omer wore his cap turned backward and that catcher's mask he was so proud of crammed down over it. Its big cage and brown padding made his face pudge up so all you could see of him was a pair of squinted eyes and his freckled cheeks.

"I think this is it," I said.

Bobby spit on the ground. "Damned Cade," he said. "He knew we was playing today. Shouldn't have tested Miss Whitlow. He knows she don't care for us playing ball."

We gazed at the other team. They had nine—not enough to lend a hand. We scuffed our feet on the ground, and spat some more.

"We could use him," I finally said, tossing a thumb toward the tree.

"The nigger boy?" Lenny Dixon said.

"You sipping the juice, Kennie?" Frank added.

I shrugged. The afternoon sun was beating down, but the heat from my teammates was more uncomfortable. "Ain't no one watching," I said. "And it's just a game."

"We ain't the Dodgers," Sammy Ben Johnson said.

That drew laughs.

I smirked, but understood. If the Dodgers and the Yankees ever managed to make it to the series, it was going to be hard rowing for a white man in Birmingham. No one around here ever would cheer a bunch of carpetbaggers, but the Dodgers were black all up and down their roster: Wills at shortstop, Gilliam at second. Tommy Davis and Willie Davis in the outfield, and Roseboro behind the plate. They were all Negroes. To root for the Dodgers in Birmingham, Alabama was like treading on quicksand with a piano on your back. Drysdale was all right, and Koufax got a pass as long as you didn't press the point, but Negroes were another thing all together.

"Ain't playing with no nigger," Lenny said. Lenny played right field, which was about as far away from shortstop as you can get on a diamond.

"Look, Lenny. I just want to win," I said. "And we ain't winning KP duty without a shortstop. Are you telling me you're okay with losing just 'cause you can't stand 150 feet from a black boy?"

Lenny glowered, but a couple of the other fellas nodded as if they hadn't thought about it quite that way. Bobby squinted at me, then gazed out over the field. No one else said anything, so I made the decision.

"You got a glove?" I said to the boy who was still leaning there against the tree.

"Can get one."

"Go on and get it, then. And hurry your ass up. Won't be no time for you to warm up."

Lenny stayed. The game went long.

When it ended, everyone went home to dinner and to sleep in our beds.

I didn't hear about the marches until Daddy turned on the radio.

I dropped the aperture cards off at the front desk and went to pick up the pages I had printed. There were birth records in there, and an arrest report. Tommy Daniels had gotten into a fight and punched a man. Motives were left to the imagination. But the prize—the golden ticket, as it were—was something else entirely.

I gathered up the missing person report, put it together with the rest, and tapped the whole thing together on the counter. The entire stack was no more than a quarter inch thick.

Lieutenant Brady walked past. She was just getting in for the day, and took a moment to throw her jacket over the back of her chair before she turned to me. Gracie Brady had helped me get access to the precinct's database the night before. She was of eastern European decent, Lithuanian, I think, but multi-generation American. I wondered if she thought of herself as Lithuanian-American, or just American.

When do you stop being a hyphen? I shrugged to myself. It didn't really matter, now, did it? You are what you are. You are what you make of yourself. You are what you let yourself be. My brain locked onto infinite permutations of this idea before Gracie Brady broke the patter.

"Good morning, Mr. Pearson," she said. "Long night?"

"Morning, Lieutenant," I said. "Yeah. Long night."

"Find what you needed?"

I raised the papers. "I think so."

She checked me out of the precinct, while I grabbed my jacket.

When I left the building a few minutes later, I found it was cold and raining. From what I saw the week I was in the city, it's always cold and raining in Philadelphia. I guess that was another lie I was telling myself, too. But it made me feel better, somehow, so I chuffed a bit as I shoved the pages under my jacket to keep them from getting soaked, and I flipped my collar up against the wet. The steps were concrete, which made my knees and ankles ache. My car was parked in a garage two blocks down, so I hunched my shoulders up and walked carefully alongside of the building the whole way, trying to use the brick as a shield from the weather.

It didn't do much good.

I suppose it's fair to say we were all breaking the law when Tommy stepped onto that field. You can't live in Birmingham, Alabama in 1963 without understanding how it is. But we needed a shortstop and Tommy said he could play—which turned out to be true enough. Tommy Daniels could play him some shortstop—and in the end I can't say as the law really had much to do with any of this whole thing.

Truth was that no one would hurt a white boy just for playing baseball. Sure, someone was likely as not to yell at us, but as long as we weren't getting too close to a black, or going out of our way to make trouble for no one about it by pushing that black on anyone, we all knew the most we had to concern ourselves with was that our daddies might come down and tan our hides a good one.

But Tommy was from up north.

He told me he was from Philly that second day when I finally broke down and said he didn't sound like a Birmingham boy. He said he was here visiting his uncle for a few weeks—which is why he was free in the afternoons. His uncle cleaned in a warehouse downtown, and worked noon to ten.

So Tommy wasn't from Birmingham.

And if you weren't from Birmingham in May of 1963, there was no way you could really know anything at all. But if you *were* from around here, if you *were* from Birmingham in May of 1963, a place where the Ku Klux Klan had its open office just a couple blocks from the cinema, and a place where those same klansmen made up a good portion of the police force, you damned well knew there are worse things that can happen to a Negro than having their daddy tear into their hide.

May 3rd:

By the time school let out that second day, I had already heard stories about the hoses and the dogs and the Negro children singing their songs as they were rounded up. I didn't think anything of it, though. There were always stories like that. This was just another. Bigger than the rest, sure. But, I don't know. They just didn't seem to matter much.

In the hallway after last bell I heard someone say they "heard the jail's so full of niggers they're dumpin' them off at the fairgrounds." And another kid say "Must be Saturday night, eh?" and everyone, including me, laughed.

When I got to the field, Lenny was already there.

So was his brother.

Clyde Dixon was older than Lenny. He was a senior at Woodlawn, and more than a bit of a rabble-rouser. He was already working at the steel plant, and probably would all his life. He and a buddy had his old Ford truck parked under the tree. It had been red at one time, but was half dirt and half rust now. The windows were rolled down, and Clyde was sitting inside with a buddy in the passenger seat, smoking a cigarette while Johnny Cash played *Ring of Fire* on the radio.

Tommy came along a pace behind, carrying his glove in his left hand and loping in his long stride. As he approached, Clyde got out of his car with his cigarette shoved into the corner of his mouth. He was carrying a shotgun that was broke-down to let him to load it if he wanted. Tommy didn't see him right away, but when he did, Clyde smiled, slammed the gun shut, and took a bead on him.

Tommy froze.

"Hey!" I yelled before my thoughts formed anything practical. For a minute I actually thought I was going to see a man shot down.

Clyde dropped the gunpoint down, and I realized then that the gun wasn't loaded.

"What you want?" he said. In his gaze, I sensed a trap. He was like a big bear or a snake sitting there, waiting for me to say something.

"Nothing," I replied. I was holding the baseball in my hands and thinking it made a shit weapon against a shotgun, and what the hell was I doing calling out Clyde Dixon when he was holding that kind of firepower.

"Don't worry," Clyde said with a slow pace. "I ain't doing nothing, either. Everyone knows you can't shoot a nigger in the daylight."

I took a breath.

"Course," he said. "Don't mean you can't do a little target practice."

"We're just playing ball," I said. "That's all."

"That's good to hear," Clyde said. He broke the barrels open again. "Cause we just happened to come here to take in a game."

Clyde gave a crooked grin and got back into the truck. His buddy lifted a brown bottle of beer, and said something that made them both crack up.

I looked at Tommy.

"Cade's got detention again," I said. "If you're playing, go on and get out there." Then I threw the ball over to Bobby.

Tommy seemed to breathe again. With a glance toward the truck, he started to get warmed up.

As Tommy stepped onto the field, I saw Clyde Dixon spit out the window of his truck.

Walking down the street in Philadelphia that morning, I couldn't recall if we won that day. For all my hardnosed nature, I couldn't recall if we won either of those days Tommy Daniels played baseball with us. All I can say for sure is that he could cover ground like no one else, and that he had an arm like a cannon. I remember turning a double play on a grounder up the middle that he back-handed to me about as well as any shortstop you'll ever see.

And I can say one more thing for sure about that evening, and that is that it rained.

I remember that because I got wet as I hoofed it home.

And I remember that rain because as I was getting wet on the way home all I could think about was the dark gleam of Clyde Dixon's shotgun, and the matching gloaming that was in his hooded eyes. He and his buddy drank while they watched the game, and they hollered and hooted at Tommy the whole way. They threw their empties into the bed of the truck, each falling with a glassy clank. On one hand the whole thing gave me an appreciation for what Jackie Robinson had gone through back in '47. On the other, it made me feel small. Like someone was watching me. I kept wondering if I needed to tell someone something, maybe my daddy. I didn't know. But when I thought about it harder, it seemed like there was nothing to say and no one to say it to. This was how life was. There was nothing for anyone to do.

And, finally, I remember that it rained that evening because at dinner I heard the truth of the day's stories—that a thousand or more Negro kids got wet that day when Bull Connor gave them the hose, and I thought of them stockpiled out at the fairgrounds, probably getting wet again.

I stepped into the parking garage and got out of the rain.

I found my car and unlocked the door. Most of the rain had beaded on my jacket, but a trickle went down my back and made me shiver as I settled into the seat. I pulled the dry pages from my chest and set them on the seat beside me. They sat there, a stack of white paper against the dark seat, whispering to me.

There are things that are hidden, and things we hide from ourselves.

May 4-8:

It rained enough that Saturday that we didn't play ball at all.

And Sunday was always an off-day in our house.

On Monday, neither Tommy Daniels nor Clyde Dixon showed up at the park. The game went on, though, same as always. By then the Birmingham jails were stuffed full of a couple thousand Negro kids.

It didn't rain at all the rest of the week, and we played baseball every day.

I looked for Tommy on Monday, worried about what to do since Cade had gotten off detention and could play. Same thing on Tuesday. I knew he was going back to Philadelphia on Wednesday, so when he didn't show I figured I would never see him again.

"Anybody seen Tommy Daniels?" I said to the boys as the first game started that Tuesday.

"Naw," Bobby Downs replied.

I frowned. "Shame he couldn't play one more time. He was good for a Negro."

Lenny laughed. "Missing your nigger boy, are you, Kennie? Cause if'n you are I'm sure I can get Clyde to get you two back together again."

The team got quiet.

"What's that supposed to mean?" I said.

"Nothing," Lenny said. "I don't know nothing about Tommy Daniels, and neither do you."

But Lenny was wrong.

I knew.

Right then I knew.

But I felt Lenny Dixon's stare and I remembered the cold aura of his brother's shotgun and I felt the rest of the guys watching me then, all of them quiet. All of us quiet. And I was weak.

But I knew.

And I never said a thing.

The history books are clear about who won the Children's Crusade of 1963. The names of the leaders are commonly spoken. Martin Luther King, Fred Shuttlesworth, Arthur Shores. A simple internet search finds them each today. But if you lived in Birmingham, Alabama in the 1960s, you know it was the *children* who exposed Bull Connor and got him stripped from office. It was the children who, by July, forced the repeal of the segregation ordinance of the Alabama code that made it a crime for all of us to play ball together those two days in May. It was the children who forced the lunch counters open and the water fountains to flow together, the children who made it legal for a black family to attend a State Fair on the same day and at the same time as a white family.

When I think about what those children did in 1963, I am humbled.

But ignorance does not die a quick death, and nothing those children did could give Birmingham a quiet transition.

The church bombing happened three months later, of course.

You've heard of it. Four little girls dead on 16th Street.

Everyone remembers them. Even today, when people look back on it they talk about Denise McNair, Addie Mae Collins, Cynthia Wesley, and Carole Robertson. Sometimes they remember to add Sarah Collins, Addie Mae's sister, who was blinded in one eye, or any of the other 19 injured in the blast.

But it's the rare report that remembers to include 16-year-old Johnny Robinson, killed by the police that same day, and 13-year-old Virgil Ware, killed by white boys in a passing car later that day just outside the city. And people don't recall three other bombs had been set in the weeks before the famous 16th Street bombing, or that two more blew the week after.

So many things get lost in history, it seems.

So many people.

A lot of that went through my mind as I drove the streets of Philadelphia. I wondered if I was crossing streets Tommy had crossed. I imagined him standing at this corner or that one. Who knew? Who would ever know?

I never did play ball much past school. Wasn't good enough, and my knees turned knobby anyway. I finished high school and graduated with a Journalism degree from the University of Alabama. First in my family to do that. I met Janice Haywood, and convinced her to take me in. We had three kids, and through it all I worked at a string of papers and wrote a book no one heard of. It was a good life, and a life I admit I muddled my way through without much thought on the past.

I am not here to say that Tommy's specter weighed over me through the years.

I am not proud to say that it did not.

I never shed a tear over the fate of Tommy Daniels, though I can at least admit he was the source of considerable unrest and confusion for me at times.

The year after I retired, though, Janice and I found ourselves in Washington D.C. visiting the Holocaust Museum. We were taking a rest when a school class walked through, chattering as the guide explained the operation of the Third Reich.

"It could never happen here," one of the girls said.

And I saw Tommy's gaze and I felt the cold burn of Clyde Dixon's shotgun.

Yes, young lady, I thought. It *can* happen here because it *did* happen here.

That's when I finally knew what I needed to do.

I had learned a thing or two about digging things up in my time, you see.

I tried to find his uncle in Birmingham, first, but he was long dead. Nothing left of the uncle's family but a brother who was dead, too, and his brother's wife who didn't know anything about him. The warehouse he worked at had changed hands several times, and I found a few folks who remembered Tommy's uncle, but they all remembered him as quiet in the way of a lot of Negroes of that age. Go along to get along, as they said back then.

I found Tommy's birth records earlier this year—made more difficult because he was brought into this world at Philadelphia State Hospital, in a psych ward where his mother was being held as mentally deranged. I picked up his trail in fits and starts, registration in a school here or a program there. But mostly Tommy Daniels was a ghost. It was almost as if he never walked the earth at all. There is every chance in the world that I was the only human being alive who had any memory of him at all.

Well, me and Clyde Dixon, anyway.

Clyde wasn't so hard to find.

And stories about Clyde weren't so hard to find, either. He was a legendary drinker in his time, and a man who wasn't afraid to make an ass of himself when the situation called for it. He'd been a Klan member, probably still was. I turned up stories of him backing up the police, and beating up whites as well as blacks. There was an epic tale of when he went to beat the pulp out of a guy for messing with a buddy's wife and picked on the wrong guy. That cost Clyde a week in the hospital.

I couldn't find anyone to talk about a shooting, though.

Until one night three weeks ago when Jimmy "Skeets" McCoy got to drinking and talking about digging a hole with Clyde one night "in the creek bank up north aside the ballfield." He told it as if digging the hole was part of a joke, as if it was a contest between the two of them, with a beer as the stake for who could dig best. The bar laughed as one when he described Clyde Dixon with enough mud on him to make him look like a goddamned nigger.

I felt it then. I caught the glances as mugs got raised.

Folks knew I was sniffing around Clyde.

Those gazes were only half an admission, but I took it to the Birmingham police, and three days later they found the bones.

It took two years to get to that point. Or maybe fifty-two if you look at it another way.

A long damned time.

When I was struggling with setbacks, Janice would ask me why I was doing it. Clyde Dixon was seventy-two years old, she said. And it was more than fifty years ago. Why worry about it? When Lenny got so mad one time that he threatened to beat me to a pulp, she worried. Wasn't it better to just let it go? she said, almost pleading. Wasn't it best to just let everything die out in its natural course?

And, yes, that would have been easiest.

But I thought of the girls in the museum, and I thought about when I looked at myself in the mirror and realized I could still picture Tommy's back-handed toss to me at second base. But mostly I remembered the feeling I had the day Lenny told me what Clyde had done.

"When history looks back," I said to her then, taking ironic pleasure in ripping-off Simon Weisenthal's famous quote, "I want people to know the Klan wasn't able to kill thousands of people and get away with it."

But inside I knew better.

I had to do this because I had known.

And because I had done nothing.

I stopped the car at a high school ball field.

The missing persons report sat on top of the pile of pages. It had been filed by a downtown YMCA employee. Tommy Daniels, 16, had been due back in Philadelphia May 9th. The report was filed the 14th by one Jeanie Majors when he hadn't showed for three days in a row. Below that was a dental notice from the jailhouse he had wound up in after his fight. He had lost the tooth there.

I had to follow it up, of course. Hopefully Jeanie Majors was still alive, and hopefully she could tell me more about Tommy Daniels.

Like baseball, so much about life is about timing, though, and I knew enough to make the call now. It felt right. I couldn't have stopped myself for all the money in the world.

I shut the engine off, and I got out of the car.

The rain had stopped, but the gravel lot was muddy.

A gate in the chain link fence was closed, but not locked. A moment later I was in the cement block dugout. I stood there for a moment looking out over the field. I breathed in the smell of fresh grass and dirt, feeling the ghosts of thousands of kids who had played here, falling prey once again to the easy target of wondering if Tommy might have been one of them. Probably not.

The wind was cold as I walked across the infield to stand at second base.

Second base was my home. It was where I felt I belonged on the baseball field.

I liked it better than shortstop because the balls came off the bat differently. Ground balls hit to short come in with an over-spinned hop that makes the ball loop along, or they come on a rope like rocket shots. Playing shortstop is about pure instinct as much as anything else. You make the right reaction the second the ball comes off the bat, or you don't get it. But balls hit to second base have cross-spin, and sometimes you get weird nubbers, or bending line drives. And when you play at second base you need to hold your own at the pivot on the double play. There's a courage you need at second base. It takes guts to straddle the bag and wait for a throw while a runner bears in on you.

I told my daddy about how I felt one day at a Barons game. I told him I wanted to be a ballplayer and I wondered if maybe I could be signed one day. And he said: "Shortstop is baseball's magician, second base is its poet."

I thought about that as I pulled out my phone. The infield dirt here in Philadelphia was more brown than Birmingham's. It stuck to the toe of my shoe as I dialed.

"Detective Bryant," the voice answered.

"Lamar," I said. "It's Kenny."

There was a pause. "What's up?"

"I got it."

"Proof that Tommy Daniels never showed back in Philadelphia?"

"More," I said.

"More?"

"A dental record."

"Son of a bitch." I could hear him sit back in his chair.

"You got the body of Tommy Daniels sitting in your evidence locker. I'll scan the files over to you today."

"If it's what you say it is, I'll have a black-and-white out there to get him this afternoon."

I broke the connection.

It was over. Above me, the sky was still overcast, still slate gray. The weather report said more rain was coming. But it was done. It was over. After all this time, Clyde Dixon was going to jail.

The band of pressure that had been twisted up inside my ribs let go, and in a single breath the field seemed to get bigger. I felt the weight of the rain on the ground. It smelled like earthworms and grass. But mostly I felt a young black boy named Tommy Daniels who I knew beyond doubt had once played shortstop, and for a minute it felt like the two of us might still be able to turn a double play.

The throw to first base looked longer than it had when I was a kid, though.

Time changes things in ways we can't predict and in ways we'll never understand.

Who knew how good Tommy could have been?

Who knew if he could have played ball as a man, or held a job? Who knew if he could have gone to school, or been a father, or had a real family? Who had known, after all, that a black boy named Tommy Daniels had ever even existed?

I did, I thought as I saw Tommy's lanky form bend down to scoop a grounder.

I knew Tommy Daniels had been here.

And I would remember.

Us vs. Them

Brigid Collins and Ron Collins

"They started it," the young man said. He pulled the collar of his leather jacket higher, then scowled. Said his name was Brian, no surname. Very Brando-like. "They got the whole group of them together and jumped us up. Cowards, there. Can't do shite without a mess of 'em around."

Brian's hair was combed into a dead-black pomp that dipped over a pair of piercing blue eyes. The odor of its Brylcreem overpowered the salt and the sea behind us. The sound of his voice rode on the cascade of waves crashing in the distance. He lit an American cigarette and blew the smoke into the afternoon air. His gang mates kept catting at us, calling him a Nancy Boy and making light of him talking to the mod girl with the notepad. It might've bothered him, but Brian had something to say and he wanted to say it.

"They don't like us," he said. "The mods, you know? Most of them, anyway. They think they're so fucking fab done up in their

threads and their bows, but they bleed just like we do. We'll see they do it often enough."

The idea that a ceramic door chime could sound like rhythm & blues to her was bonkers, but—as Linda stepped off the beachside street and into the flowery miasma of Mame's Boutique—the clatter called up echoes of the band she'd heard the night before.

Blame it on a bucketload of coffee and the bennie she'd taken to wake up—which was made necessary by the purple hearts she'd downed to keep out late the night before, and the mandie she'd dropped to finally get into the sack.

It had been worth it, though.

The band called themselves the Who these days, though she knew them as the High Numbers. She wasn't sure the new name worked, but she liked dancing to their music, and she liked that they played "I'm the Face" no matter what they called themselves. They'd been at the Florida Room, and the party'd been fabulous—especially given the ruckus on the beach earlier. Bobbies and rockers had both beat up on the boys, and the boys had returned as good as they got before the bobbies carted several off (with the unfortunate inclusion of Linda's good friend Peter, who'd only been guilty of being in the wrong place at the wrong time).

Several of the boys at the club last night had still been hyper from the rumble, some wearing green-black shiners and puffed-up lips, dancing even more outrageously than they usually did. Others, the calmer ones with set jaws and slit gazes, gave warnings of getting their pound of flesh back. *It's a fucking war,* they'd said. *It happened at Margate and Broadstairs, too.* Linda always thought fighting to be a silly game, but being in the Florida Room last night felt different. She was a mod after all. Brighton Beach was their home, and the boys had done their best to defend it. Everyone else felt it, too. The crowd had been as raw as the rakishly loud music.

God, she couldn't wait to tell Pamela and Peter what a smasher of a show they'd missed.

Of course, given the headache raging through her temples, not even the door chime could make her feel like dancing this early in the day. A Sunday no less.

Linda pulled a notepad from her handbag.

This column wouldn't be gathering Pulitzers anytime soon—and if anyone at her paper had seen anything even remotely resembling "fashion" since Hedy Lamarr stopped making films they'd never have sent her *here*—but it paid bills and kept her out of her parents' flat. Sleep-starved or not, it was time to go to work.

Despite yesterday's riots, the place was doing good business—as well it should, being Whitsun holiday.

The boutique was small, with tightly spaced floor racks smashed full of discount dresses and beach wraps, half of which would later be left draped over errant lounge chairs. The air was clotted with lilac freshener and a hint of stale ciggies. Sand crunched under her simple flats, and a decrepit radio behind the cashier spewed war-time swing. The music made Linda frown. The war was twenty years gone, people. Time moves on. Things change.

She shouldn't have been surprised at the selection, though. The chances of hearing anything like the Boys, the Eyes, or even the Who in a cookie-cutter beach boutique like Mame's were about as good as seeing the Queen on a Vespa.

Wading through the "music," she sidestepped a trio of old birds tittering over summery-yet-modest dresses. Their perfume reeked of Eau de Old Lady *(Dear God, let me die before I wear something like that).* The fragrance made her itch with the fact that she was wearing her most respectable—according to Mr. Deitz anyway—white blouse and charcoal gray skirt. The blouse's collar was lacey like her mum always went for, the sleeves embroidered in a pattern straight out of the 30s. Worse, the ensemble was topped with a navy pillbox, a most doleful hat that made it look like her hair was tucked up and under rather than cut short and sporty.

She'd rather be on the boardwalk in her new jacket and the suede boots she'd gotten in London last week with Pamela. That get-up would have drawn glances from the scooter boys she'd spotted on her way here.

She could play nice with the adults, though.

Usually, anyway.

Though to be honest, when the gray-haired lady perched behind the counter (Mame Lancaster herself?) stared down her nose (*despite* the respectable skirt and hat), she found herself fighting an urge to be sassy. "Excuse me," Linda said instead. "I'm Linda Brennan, from the *Daily News*, my editor spoke on the phone?"

"Oh, thank God. I thought you were with one of those dreadful hooligans."

"No, ma'am."

Outside, three rockers raced past on motorcycles bleating loud enough to rattle the shop's windows.

Mame scowled, then turned back, her gaze suddenly softer. "It's nice to see people your age taking an interest in productive activities." She peered more closely at Linda, tilting her head. "I didn't expect a lassie, though."

A wave of indignation filled Linda's mind.

"No, ma'am, I suppose you wouldn't."

As she considered adding something more inappropriate, a nearby police klaxon blared loud enough that everyone in the boutique jumped.

Outside the windowfront people were running down the beach.

Muffled voices rose, and a woman screamed. A constable raced down the sidewalk holding his truncheon with one hand and his white helmet to his head with the other.

Bloody hell, Linda thought. *It's happening again.*

Despite boys being busted up and arrested, the fights from yesterday were happening again.

A surge of energy reminded her of last night, and she clutched her notepad tighter.

These were her people. This was her beach.

She had to be there.

Without thinking, Linda dashed through the shop.

Cars on King's Road were stopped to take in the commotion, causing others to honk their horns. The tang of the ocean mixed with fish and chips from shops down the street. On the beach itself, fists were flying. Scrums that looked like lads playing rugby rolled across the sand, boys kicking boys with walloping whumpfs. She saw blood on faces. Uniformed police ringed the mass, some beating on the boys, others waiting to see who was going to emerge victorious, presumably to arrest them all later.

Before she knew it, she'd raced across the street, causing tires to squeal and more horns to blare.

She'd nearly reached the sand when someone crashed into her.

She spun as she fell. The impact with the sidewalk took her breath. Sound merged to a confusing pulse as she pushed herself to a sitting position. She had lost her notepad. Her hat had fallen off. The meat of her right hand was raw from the fall, the pain started a moment later.

"Linda?" the voice seemed familiar.

"Pamela?"

Linda's friend clung to the lamppost she'd used to keep from falling. She was taller than Linda, prettier too. Blonde and trim. She wore a bright green scooter dress and a shoulder bag that dangled off kilter. Her hair, normally set to perfection, was also mussed.

"Are you okay?" Pamela said as she helped Linda up.

"I'm fine," she replied, still in a bit of a fog.

A police whistle down the beach broke her daze.

It was only then that she really saw Pamela, the spikes of her slingback heels half buried in the sand, her hair mussed by much more than the crashing they'd had, her face dark as a cloud, her eyes puffy, her mascara smeared and running.

"What's happening?" Linda said. "Have you been crying?"

"It's Peter," Pamela replied.

"What?" Linda said, turning to look for Peter in the mass of fighting boys.

If there was a poster boy for maximum pacifism, Peter Traffigan was it. Slight and graceful, reserved and painfully shy,

Peter was one of those beautiful boys who drew gazes just sitting in a corner. That he could wear anything from a blazer to a pullover and still break your heart just made it worse. She'd heard Peter had been taken to the station yesterday because *Jimmy* had pulled him into the mess, but even the densest copper would see there was no fight in Peter and immediately let him go.

She looked over the beach. This close, the scuffle didn't seem as bad as yesterday's was made out, but boys were still getting hurt.

"I don't see him," Linda said.

Pamela's hand clamped onto Linda's arm. "He's gone, Linda."

"Gone?" Pamela's blotched face re-registered. "Oh, God. You mean Peter's actually missing?"

Pamela nodded, a sob sticking in her throat. She put her hand over her mouth and burst into what were certainly not her first tears of the day.

"What happened?"

"We were supposed to go to the show last night. I rang him up and went by his flat both last night and this morning." she said. "I've checked the parks and the clubs. Even went to the bank."

"It's holiday Sunday," Linda said. "He wouldn't be working."

"I checked anyway," Pamela said.

Peter. Missing. Anger at the idea nearly consumed her.

"You're the only one I know to come to. You're a reporter, right? You can find things out?"

"What do you mean?"

"He had a date, Linda. He wouldn't say who it was, but I think he was meeting someone." Pamela's face took a set. "Someone special, you know?"

Yes. Linda did know.

Pamela drew a breath. "And there's a dead boy," she said, her eyes shining with anguish. The pressure of her hand on Linda's arm grew tight as a tourniquet. "You heard it, right? A boy from London dead at Saltdean last night?"

A brace of fear chilled her spine.

Peter often went to the cliffs when he had someone special with him. If he was meeting someone, Saltdean would be the place.

She turned on a heel and strained to find the one person who might know something about what happened.

"They started it," the young man said. "But what do you expect from a whole fucking flight of greasers?"

Jimmy Smith was tall and thin, with his dark hair trimmed short. He was a lad first from Hampton who came to town for the club scene, which made sense. For those of the right mind, Brighton is a place second only to Soho. It's a city filled with proper businesses and men of regal bearing, so it's got money. But it's also a place where other money comes to play, and where a young person can make a spot for themselves. The scene here is a buzz so low you can forget it's there, but if you're listening it's strong and clear. Brighton's clubs, beaches, and vacation-rich sense of impermanence call to anyone with a mod sensibility. It is not, after all, a place you want to be seen wearing last week's ads.

He leaned against a post at the corner of Ship and Kings, wearing a suit that looked like it came straight from Carnaby Street. He wore it well and proper, too. Top button clasped, blue shirt underneath with a pressed collar, a thin black tie, and a pair of dark glasses that couldn't hide the swelling from his left eye. Exposure didn't seem to bother him, though. I assumed that if the beachy sun wasn't so bright and the day wasn't so early, he'd probably be just as happy to show the shiner off, that if he could rip the wound from his cheekbone he'd paste it on the front of the blue and green Lambretta he'd parked at the side of the street— probably at the top of the windshield for everyone to see.

"I've seen you around the clubs, haven't I?" he asked as I jotted notes.

The question annoyed me, though I tried not to show it. Yes, I'd met Jimmy before. Several times, though not for long, and most of those times his eyes had been bright with speed and drink. Give him a pass, I thought.

I said I lived here and that I would be at the Florida Room to see the Who again at the All-Nite Rave—their last gig of the weekend.

He smiled wide, then, his toothy whiteness gleaming in the afternoon sun.

Yes, I thought. The shiner was a badge. And not a bad one.

"Well, then, missy," he said. "That means we've both got brains enough to know a mod's never going to go kiss off from a fight, am I right?"

It was my turn to smile.

"Make sure you get that down right, though. When you're doing your reporting, tell everyone that even though we gave it a good and proper ending, they're the ones that started it."

Running down the beach, Linda was finally happy for the flats.

This close to the ocean, waves were a constant hiss and the screams of gulls sounded like men at a boxing match. Gulps of air hurt her lungs as she raced across the beach, her feet sliding in loose sand until she came to the nearest pod of shouting, shoving boys—a few of which she walloped with the broad side of her heavy and oh-so-respectable handbag, leaving the lads on their arses as she slipped through the mass of fighters.

Jimmy was as impossible to miss as Peter, but for opposite reasons.

He was a big boy, a footballer with the muscles to prove it. He found these kinds of fights like a pigeon finds its way home, unthinkingly attracted by some mystical magnetism in his tiny brain. This was why the pairing of Peter and Jimmy had been so odd in the first place. Big and small. Rugged and beautiful. Action and intellect. It had been clever fun to watch them together, even when it was so obviously a match doomed from the beginning.

She found him right where she expected: tangled with a pair of rockers he'd taken a fancy to tussling with before.

"Oi!" she yelled. "Clear off!"

A couple rockers and a mod boy stepped back, obviously stunned by the sight of a girl entering the fray, even one with her teeth bared and her handbag swinging like a cudgel. A moment later they set to whaling on each other once again.

"I said to clear the fuck off!" she yelled, kicking the shin of a denim-clad greaser.

The whole cluster nearby straightened up, brushing hair from their eyes and glaring at her from under tousled bangs and flopping pompadours.

She ignored them and squeezed through to arrive at a final chaotic mess.

Jimmy held his stance in the middle of the scrum, pounding on a rocker who'd tumbled to the ground. The tatters of his unbuttoned jacket flapped in the wind. His tie was as askew as his unkempt hair. His knees bent as he kicked the boy, and his knuckles dripped blood onto the sand. A wild gleam shone in his eyes, pupils dilated and the whites running with crimsoned veins that said dexies and hard liquor. He'd freshened the shiner on his left eye, and his busted grimace was laced with scarlet as he screamed his own stream of profanity.

"Jimmy Smith!" she yelled as she stepped closer.

Jimmy swung wildly at a kid who happened to be a mod. He lurched with the punch, dropping to one knee, then staggering to pick himself up. This close, it was obvious Jimmy was so far gone he could barely stand.

"Fahking greasehead!" he screamed, and kicked wildly as a rocker came into view.

Linda grabbed his tie and yanked him forward. "Come on."

"Wha-th-bloody hell'r ya—" Jimmy said before the tie cut his words to a squawk. His breath was as raw as his voice.

She grabbed his arm and yanked harder, nearly falling as his weight crashed into her.

"Wha-tha-fahk d'you think you're doin', Laura?" Jimmy said as she guided him out of the scrum. He nearly toppled again as she pushed him through the crowd.

"There'd better be enough of you left to pummel," she said, giving him a final shove that made him fall to his knees. She towered over him, feeling the power of the ocean wind in her hair as her chest rose and fell with her exertion. Her blood was up, and she gritted her teeth to get control of herself.

"Wha-the-hell, Laura!"

"Shut up!" Linda said, somehow keeping from slapping him. "What happened to Peter last night, Jimmy?

"Peter!" Jimmy moaned. The smell of old gin was thick, but Jimmy's eyes teared up in a way that made the crimson veins glow, then he fell forward and wrapped his arms around her as he buried his head against her hip.

"You were with him at the fight," she said, creating separation. "What happened?"

"Fahking greaser! He's the one what did it."

"What greaser, Jimmy? Did what?"

Jimmy's eyes goggled, and his face went purple. "Oh, *fahk*off, yah little bitch. Fahkoff yah wanna know how Peter got done, I say jess go talk to that cocked-up greaser arsehole what always follows us 'round." He got to his feet, and shook his finger so close to her face she was suddenly afraid. "Where is tha bleedin' pretty-boy today, eh? Not here, is he?" He tried to step away, but stumbled. "I beat his face right an' proper yesterday. Don't think I won't put a right end on it, even if I have ta deal his share to the rest of these filthy greasers."

He stood straight, balled his fists, and took a step toward the scrum.

A dark blue form swooped in as if from nowhere, a portly bobby with billy club at the ready. With surprise on his side, the copper wrapped the weapon around Jimmy's chest and threw him to the ground, then whacked him three times across the shoulder so hard that Linda thought she heard bone cracking.

Jimmy wailed and struggled to stand up, so the cop hit him again.

This time Jimmy stayed still, moaning while a fresh stream of blood ran into the sand.

"Appreciate you dragging this one out, ma'am. I had my eye on him earlier," the constable said, wheezing through his nose. He was an older man, sporting a bristly mustache shot with grey and wearing at least forty pounds more than police regulations called for.

"Why'd you have to do that?" she said, struggling to absorb the violence she'd seen.

"We'll take it from here, though."

Linda saw his name plate read "Carmichael."

"Get off my fahking beach!" Jimmy suddenly burst out at a group of gawkers.

Carmichael whacked him two more times, then got him into handcuffs.

A moment later, he'd dragged Jimmy away, leaving Linda to stand alone among the scuffles that were continuing up and down the beach. She felt cold despite the sun that beat on her face, numb as she absorbed the moment. The salty breeze tousled her not-so-sporty hair. Her palm prickled where Jimmy's tie had rubbed her raw.

"I can't believe that just happened."

The crunch of footsteps in sand broke her quiet. Linda turned to find Pamela shading her eyes.

In the wake of Jimmy's fury, her own came to a more manageable squall.

Suddenly she wanted her notepad.

Her gaze went to the sandy spot where she and Pamela had first crashed into each other. Not finding the notepad, she felt somehow naked.

"You think Jimmy knows something?" Pamela said, gesturing to where Jimmy had lain moments before.

Linda nodded. Jimmy knew something all right, and it had wound him up good and tight. Too good and too tight. Everyone who knew that Jimmy and Peter had once been together knew Jimmy'd never really given up on it. He'd gotten Peter dragged into the station, after all. Maybe that was on purpose?

Once Jimmy cooled down he'd be more likely to tell her what he saw. In the meantime, she needed another lead.

"What do you know about a greaser following Peter around?" she said.

"A Teddy Boy?"

"Yeah, Peter and a rocker."

Pamela shrugged. "Nothing, I guess. But you know Peter."

Linda drew a resolved breath. Yes, she knew Peter. It wasn't that he didn't have standards—though you could be forgiven for thinking so, with Jimmy as exhibit A—it was that Peter could accept anyone, even a biker with slicked-back hair. He saw things in ways no one else did.

"You said they found the boy in Saltdean?"

"Yes," Pamela said. "On the beach under the cliffs."

"All right then," Linda replied. She looked down the way. Saltdean was five miles east. "Do you know anyone with a scooter?"

Pamela smiled for the first time of the day.

"I doubt that Jimmy'll be using his."

Before leaving, Linda went to her flat to change. The afternoon edition of the paper lay on her front mat. She scooped it up and fumbled to unlock her door.

Maybe it was her imagination that lent the newsprint its feeling of warmth, but she liked thumbing through the pages. That was the thing about newspapers for her. They held a timeless aura and a covert sense of promise that made them feel like briefs from MI6.

The dead boy in Saltdean had been identified, a kid named Barry Prior.

A terrible accident, the paper suggested.

Of Peter, however, there was nothing.

"You can't be missing if you never existed in the first place, now, can you?" she said to herself, feeling a dusting of anger.

Distractedly, she threw on a snug blouse in pale green, khaki slacks, and a pair of brown leather boots. To this she added a scarf that went swimmingly with the shirt. Appropriate riding clothes, she thought. Very aviator. She considered a jacket, then decided to let it go, arguing that it couldn't take all day to scour Saltdean, so she'd be home before it got too cold, but realizing just as well that the look made her feel more daring without it.

The right outfit made her feel things, and this one made her feel like she was going to find Peter alive and well.

She glanced at the headlines once again.

They reported only one dead boy, after all, so that's what was going to happen. She was going to find Peter holed up in a flat with some boy, scold him, and bring him back to Brighton to be rested and ready for the rave tomorrow evening.

But the image of Pamela's face argued against her, mascara running and dread crinkling the corners of her lips.

Yah wanna know how Peter got done, I say jess go talk to that cocked-up greaser ...

Yah wanna know how Peter got done...go talk to that greaser arsehole

Wanna know how Peter

Got done

Leaving the paper in a crumpled pile on her bedroom floor, she went to collect her ride.

To be honest, Linda preferred the Vespa, but borrowers couldn't be choosers. She hopped on Jimmy's Lambretta and took off, pleased that its blue side panels and green upper fit the rest of her look.

As the road led her out of town, she imagined she was in a movie and the soundtrack was the Eyes' "When the Night Falls."

Her fear for Peter loomed ahead, but for the moment the feel of the engine below her and the whine of the tires gave her a sense of freedom she liked. Her hands were bare over the handlebars because when she checked the compartment between the front shield and the handlebars, she found Jimmy had lost one of the fancy gloves the company sold with the scooter—possibly the one reason she would ever consider buying the Lambretta over a Vespa once she'd saved up enough to get her own ride. At first, she considered wearing just the one glove but decided that would be weird, so instead she suffered the chill against her knuckles as the scooter made its way over the coastal road—rocky inland to her left, rolling waves of the Channel on the right.

As she left Brighton proper, the idea that she was working on something important brought her an odd sense of strength. She was young, nearly twenty years old, and living in a flat of her own, but until now she'd only really felt like a larger version of herself as a kid. Maybe that was because of how her dad had scoffed when she moved out.

"You'll be back," he'd said. "We'll see if we take ya in."

Linda gripped the handles harder, twisting the throttle to run faster.

Her dad had been in the war, but her mum was the only one to talk about it.

Linda glanced to the sky above and remembered her mum in the kitchen, mashing potatoes for their dinner and describing how she watched planes fly over the city and across the water, Nazi bombers with their mottled bodies and RAF Spitfires with their bright roundels, their engines growling in the sky with sound she felt in her stomach. Her mother's fists pounded harder when she talked about bombs that destroyed houses and set the gasworks on fire, killing men, women, and children all the same.

It was hard to think of that now. Hard to imagine Compton Street filled with glass from blown-out windows, and other buildings blown to bits. Hard to think of years with the city closed and the beaches wired and mined. She always thought she understood why her father was like he was, but after seeing the boys on the beach she wasn't so sure.

Maybe she'd never be able to really understand him.

Not that it mattered anymore. She'd torched that bridge good and proper.

Linda thought about the position she'd put her mum in by leaving as she did. Maybe Vivien Brennan actually loved her husband and maybe she didn't, but she was still a loyal British housewife. She stood with him as Linda walked out the door even though Linda knew it tore her to shreds when she did.

Now Linda was writing a fashion column she despised and spending all her free time going to clubs, dancing, and taking the little pills and extra helpers she needed to keep going. It was a strange life. Strange to her father's sensibilities, at least, though she thought her mum would understand.

But there was something here for her.

Something deeper than what she was doing.

Something that dug under her skin when she was alone like she was right now, the land rolling past, the Lambretta's vibration warming her, and the rhythm of the ocean sliding underneath the steady hum of the scooter's little engine. The mod life meant something. There were standards here, and rules you could follow. The boys and young ladies were all like her, too. She could talk to them.

Then there was the music.

She'd had a conversation with Pamela once.

"You know you're better than this," Pamela had said after reading one of her columns.

"What do you mean?"

"You should write something real."

"Like what?"

"Like. I don't know. What's important to you?"

"Fashion is important to me."

Pamela's crossed eyes and extended tongue made Linda laugh.

"No one cares what Madame Minerva Thachett wore to her granddaughter's fifth birthday," Pamela replied. "Least of all you."

"So, what should I write about?"

"The Eyes, maybe? Buster Lennox and the Trotters?"

Linda snorted. "No one wants to hear what I've got to say about music."

It got quiet for a few too many beats. Linda looked at Pamela, who wore an expression of some hurt.

Pamela said, "I do."

As the road wound past Rottingdean and the old hotel on the beach, Linda thought again about the newspaper.

Its barebones mention of poor Barry Prior and its lack of anything about Peter mingled with the image of the billy club descending on Jimmy Smith. The pairing unsettled her. She felt a guitar riff from the night before and saw boys dancing and crashing into each other.

She got queasy enough that she had to pull over and catch her breath.

Sitting on the side of a narrow road along the southern coast, gulping breaths of sea salt and exhaust fumes, she was struck by the juxtaposition of these two events as they appeared in print.

What should a good journalist do with those things? Whose story should she tell? Those questions felt more professional than any she'd asked while working on her insipid "fashion" column.

There was a story here.

A real one.

There was the fact that Peter, like Jimmy, had come to Brighton on his own and, also like Jimmy, had no one to report him missing other than a few friends who might well consider his absence a case of him running off on an adventure. Add to this that Peter, Jimmy, and maybe even this greaseball rocker Jimmy was so jealous of were walking criminals for the simple fact that they liked people of their own sex, and you'd see Peter lived in an entirely different and secret world.

Then there was Jimmy, who forced Peter to watch him beat on rockers just to pump himself up.

There was Pamela, and music. Clothes. Scooters. Bikes. Rockers. Skinheads. Punks. The Beatles. The Who. The idea that a young woman could be alone on a scooter on the highway would scare her father, but for her it meant the world was bigger than before. You could hop on a jet today and in ten hours be in America, or Australia, or Japan.

Yes, she'd been dismissive of Pamela's suggestions, but the thought of covering the Brighton Beach fashion beat the rest of her life made her want to vomit.

She lingered a few moments more, looking out over the Channel, then started eastward again.

As she crossed into Saltdean, she knew only one thing for certain. Though the ride had taken only ten minutes, Linda Brennan was a different person now than when she'd left Brighton.

Something about Saltdean gave Linda a gray feeling. It was more than the rainclouds building far out to sea and the blustering wind coming off the bluffs. Saltdean was a workaday city. A place where people lived more than vacationed. She'd been here before, of course, had enjoyed coming for tea and biscuits with her friends. But now the place felt empty. Like it was missing something, or maybe hiding something. Instead of vague memories of sunnier days, Saltdean reeked of isolation and solitude.

As if to confirm her unease, Jimmy's Lambretta issued a handful of sputtering coughs as she rolled into town. Its struggles made her consider going straight to the cliffs, which were a bit further east, but it was well past lunchtime and she was hungry. Besides, she wanted to talk to people in places she knew Peter frequented. She dropped the Lambretta's speed and hoped the engine would hold out.

The Irish girl running the tea shop Linda ate in said she knew of Peter.

"I saw him a few days ago. Pale young lad, isn't he? Wears a pair of glasses? Has a hard time with numbers, though, don't he?" she said.

"No," Linda said, heart sinking. "He's quite good with numbers."

"Ah. Haven't seen him, then. Hope you find him soon, though!"

"I'll keep looking," Linda said, and thanked her.

She drew a blank with men at a pub, though they asked her to join them.

The police were less help than the men.

The woman who ran the B&B Peter often stayed at played coy until she was convinced Linda was really a friend, then confessed he used her rooms, but said he hadn't been in for a couple weeks. "I hope he's well," she said as Linda left. "Tell him we've got in the raspberry jam he loves so much."

Her final stop was the newspaper.

"Easy case to cover," the reporter said. "It was late night, after three, they say. The boy just fell. Probably got up to ... ah ... relieve himself, and just fell. Made a bloody mess at the bottom of the rocks."

The reporter was in the dark when Linda asked about Peter.

Standing now at the side of the street just outside the office, Linda let out a rattling sigh.

She was out of leads.

Worse, she was having a hard time fighting the voice that kept suggesting she was wrong about Peter coming here, that maybe the paper hadn't reported on him simply because he hadn't been here at all.

For a minute she thought of the laugh she and Pamela would have when he showed up after having taken off north for the holiday. But that didn't feel right. Peter would have said something. Told someone.

She couldn't give up.

He had to be somewhere, and her gut still told her that somewhere was Saltdean.

She swung a leg over the scooter, uncertain where she was headed next. She'd barely settled in when a trio of boys stepped out of the police station ahead of her.

They were proper mods, jackets and shirts under parkas and anoraks. They wore their hair neat. Their faces were young, though, almost too young to be part of her crowd. Despite this, dark lines drawn into their sallow cheekbones gave them an artificial hint of age. They were a subdued bunch, too. Compared to the scooter boys she'd watched on the beach a few hours ago, these boys looked like they'd had the fight sucked out of them. All three walked as if there was weight on their shoulders as they slouched their way to a group of scooters across the street.

Three boys, she thought. Four scooters.

The meaning of this hit her hard.

Ditching her ride, Linda moved towards the boys. "Hello there."

The trio turned as one. The closest cleared his throat. "Yeah?"

Linda glanced at the unclaimed scooter. "I read about Barry. He was your friend, wasn't he?"

The one who'd spoken jerked his head away. The one on his left twisted his mouth like some horrible whoop was fighting to emerge. The other looked at Linda, his face turning pale in the sunlight.

"I'm looking for someone," she said. "A friend missing since yesterday. I wondered if you'd seen him?"

The boys exchanged glances and pushed their fists down into their parkas.

"He's one of us," Linda said, hoping she didn't sound too desperate, then she launched into her description of Peter with even more drive than she'd given every shop owner in town, continuing as if the force of her words alone could keep them from saying they hadn't seen Peter at all. This had to work. She couldn't take another dud.

"We all see after each other, right?" she said. "Take after each other when there's no one else? His name's Peter Traffigan. I'm hoping you can tell me about him."

When she ran out of words she waited.

"We saw him last night," the one finally said. "He was with us up on the bluff."

"He was a friend of Barry's from their schooling," the boy on the left added in.

"Friends?" Linda asked with an edge to her voice.

"Barry liked girls," the third said.

"I see," Linda replied.

"They were talking all night, though. Catching up, you know? Stayed up later than us. We didn't tell about him, though, because you know how people would get."

Linda nodded. "Yes, I do."

"We didn't want that on Barry's mum."

Linda nodded. True or not, the taint of having a homosexual in the family would be hard to handle at any time. Still, she had to find Peter.

"Where did Peter go?" Linda said.

"Can't say." He shrugged. "He was gone when we woke up."

Linda pressed her lips together.

"Thanks, and I'm sorry for your friend. Are you going to stay for the rave tomorrow?"

"We'll be packing up and going home."

The three stared at the extra scooter as if presented by some impossible problem of complex calculus.

"Can I get your names?" she said. "In case I have questions later?"

They hesitated.

"I'll be discreet. Everything off the record."

Another set of exchanged glances later she had their names, addresses, and telephone numbers.

As she walked back to the Lambretta, Linda ran her hand through her windblown hair and thought about the cliffs that would have to be her last destination. The Telscombe Cliffs were a rocky outcrop of greened-up hills that jutted out into the ocean a quarter mile east. She'd been there several times. It was a quiet place, unassuming, a little spot in the universe that was all on its own. She got a hint of Peter then, his hair blowing in the salt wind. The haunted gaze of the three boys chased that away.

Please, God, don't make me have to look like them, she thought as she kicked the Lambretta to life.

She turned the scooter in the middle of the street and waved as she drove by the boys. The part of her assembling this story wanted to watch them until they figured out how they were going to drive away. Because once they managed that trick, they were going to have to work on the problem of balancing the tragic ending of Barry Prior's story. How do you do that, she thought.

How do you deal with a dead boy?

The cliffs were only a short distance away, but the Lambretta's engine sputter grew harsher and the machine lost more power. She glanced at the fuel gauge. It read full enough. Still, the scooter sounded like it would expire on the spot.

Another few yards and she gave up and pulled over.

The motor wound down with a whine.

For a mod who loved his scooter so much he painted up the outside, Jimmy apparently took shit care of its innards.

Pushing the scooter up the last bit of road, Linda spoke completely unladylike language. Finding a mechanic on Sunday would be difficult enough, but finding one during holiday would be a bloody miracle.

One problem at a time, though.

At this time of day, nearing evening and with the colder winds coming, she'd expected to have the place to herself. But a motorbike was parked on the gravel pullout, its chrome gleaming in the dimming daylight.

Linda left the Lambretta beside the bike, leaning on its stand.

The smell of salt was sharper here. The calling of the gulls was more somber, cries for companionship rather than squabbling over food. The wind buffeted her cheeks and sent her scarf whipping.

A lone figure sat on the ground at the end of the bluff.

She walked toward him, passing where the reporter said Barry Prior had fallen to his death.

At first all Linda could see of the figure was the smooth leather of his jacket, which was painted with a fading Union Jack. His head was down, his arms clasped around his knees. For all he moved, he might have been a statue carved from a limestone boulder, dark with lichen. As she drew near, she saw his denim dungarees and a knife sheathed high on his hip, belted toward the back. A rocker, she thought for an incongruous moment. A rocker here on Saltdean. The idea had never crossed her mind.

Something glinted from the scrub grass beside him. A step later she saw it was a silver flask.

She didn't try to be quiet, but she was nearly beside him before he snapped his head around. For just an instant, an expression of hope softened his tough-guy face. His blue eyes danced like waves beyond the cliff.

Then she registered, and his shoulders fell.

He turned back to the ocean.

Linda was surprised he didn't turn hostile. She was obviously a mod and, worse, a mod *girl*. Rockers weren't known for their regard of either, and given the events of the weekend, she'd assume the worst. But this boy just let out a breath and glanced over his shoulder when she hung back, as if to ask why she hadn't sat down yet.

So she did, hunching against the wind, pulling her scarf up and pushing her hands into her pockets. Tufts of grass prickled her skin through her slacks. This close, she felt the warmth of his arm. The smells of Brylcreem, leather, and sweat were strong.

Finally, Linda said, "It looks like we were both hoping to find someone else here."

The rocker's gaze stayed on the horizon while he reached for the flask. "Yeah," he said, unscrewing the cap.

He took a sloshy drink, then handed it to her.

Linda grimaced. Whisky. Not her favorite, but she took a drink then handed it back.

The boy screwed the cap on and dropped it back to the grass.

"I'm Linda," she said, pushing her fists deeper into her pockets. It was getting cold.

"Brian."

She nodded. She knew him, of course. Not that they'd ever spoken. But she'd seen him. The only way she could have recognized him harder was if she were watching Jimmy put him in a headlock. The image brought back Jimmy's drunken tirade.

"Did you see Peter here?" she said, feeling awkward as the question fell out of her mouth. "I won't tell anyone, you know. If you did, I wouldn't tell. I'm worried for him, though. Please tell me if you saw him."

In the moment it took Brian to respond, an entire narrative spun through Linda's mind. Brian came here to meet his boyfriend only to find Peter and Barry together. Maybe he was drunk or high on speed. Rockers smoked lots of marijuana. Maybe it was that. Or maybe he was just torn up with jealousy. In a rage he pushed the pair off the cliffs. Now here he was, dealing with it.

The thought of his knife sent a chill down her spine that had nothing to do with the wind.

"Didn't see him," Brian said with a grimace. He spun the cap on his flask and took a long pull. "We were supposed to meet up, but he never showed."

He handed her the flask. She took another sip.

"I heard he was here," she said. "Yesterday evening, maybe."

"He never showed."

"A boy died here last night?"

"I heard."

"A mod, you know? One of ours."

"'msorry."

"I didn't know him. Reporter said he went over right about there." She pointed to the spot.

Then they sat silent again, listening to the gulls above and the waves crashing below.

Suddenly, Brian let his forehead hit his knees again. "Ah, fuck."

He stood, brushed dirt from his pants, then pulled his jacket straight. He picked up his flask and offered a hand to Linda.

"You and I both know we've got to take a look, right?"

She took Brian's hand and continued holding it as they neared the edge. Standing at the precipice gave her a sense of vertigo strong enough to make her clasp it tighter. He let her lean into him, and she braced her other hand high over his elbow, feeling the firmness of his flesh, feeling the fact that, rocker or not, this was a human body beside her.

Together they peered over the cliff.

The beach below was cloaked in shadow, but no shadow could hide the rocky teeth of the landing. A person falling here would stand no chance.

"Groty," Brian said, stepping back.

Linda took a breath, then let it out. "Yes," she said. "Maximum grotesque."

Clearly if Peter had gone over the cliff here, the authorities would have found him. But the bluff jutted into the Channel like a rocky thumb. Brian walked around the precipice, heading toward the point farthest south, farthest into the waters. He stopped at spots, leaning over the ledge to peer down.

Linda followed suit.

She took in the ground around them, looking for bent grasses or ruts in the sandy rock up high on the bluff tower. Signs of struggle. Signs of anything, really.

There was a place at the point where a boot heel could have dug down, another place where maybe thicket had been bent over by too much weight.

Silently, they peered over the edge again.

Water crashed against sheer rock below, spraying clouds of white foam up into the air. The roaring of the waves overwhelmed her. The taste of salt came, salt and sulfur and fear and flailing. There was no beach here. No sand. A boy who fell into these churning waves might well be sucked down into the guts of the ocean never to be seen again.

"Dear God," she said, her voice clutching like a bone in her throat.

"What is that?"

Brian pointed down the cliff a bit where something was stuck, too small to make out in the light. A clutch of fabric, maybe? Torn from a pant or a jacket?

"Brace me," Brian said as he knelt.

Linda took his hand and leaned back to lever his reach as he leaned over the precipice. She felt his weight against hers. A cold wind blew off the sea. Her scarf nearly flew from her neck.

He gave a grunt, then came up. Standing, he held something out.

She reached for it, knowing what it was from touch alone.

Slowly, though, she looked down to confirm.

A single glove, with the Lambretta shield on it.

"It's all these kids what are to blame, beggin' your pardon, miss," said Officer Carmichael. He stood at the back of the pier, watching with narrowed eyes as a trio of mods had a laugh down at the other end. He wore his dark blue uniform as prim and proper as any mod, and he kept his shoulders back and his barrel chest thrust forward as if that, rather than his badge or his truncheon, was where he carried that authority of his. He must have known he couldn't carry it in his face. Even though he was a couple decades my senior, I had a hard time managing a proper expression of respect.

His white helmet gleamed bright in the sun, though.

I asked if he could elaborate on his accusation.

"It's the whole lot of 'em," he said. "You ask some other lads on the force and one might say it's your mod rabble, or another'll say it's the rockers. But it's the whole lot, and no mistake. Ungrateful beasts, all of them. Think they're immortal."

He threw another glare down the pier. The mods were on the pilings, pretending to push one another off. His attention was diverted by the roar of motorbikes as a pair of rockers drove along the street, jeering at us, the mod girl and the police officer.

"Yes, they think they're all immortal," Carmichael said, "and they'll kill themselves to prove it, they will. Selfish. If it weren't for the property damage, I'd say let 'em bash each other to bits. Save everyone a whole lot of grief."

Brian fixed her scooter, saying it was the fuel filter clogged up.

"Can't really solve that," he said, wiping the petrol from his hand, "but I took it out so it'll go. You'll need a new one."

She thanked him, and they got on their way.

They made quite the sight rolling down the coastal road, she supposed, he beside her like some kind of oily knight in chrome armor, she sitting upright and prim with her feet resting on the scooter's wide floorboard and her scarf flying behind.

Though it was cold now, she couldn't bring herself to wear the gloves.

The chill made her wish she'd chosen the jacket, though. It struck her that wearing it would have given an even more surreal flavor to the image of the rocker boy and mod skirt rolling into town together. But that image was broken when, a half mile out of Brighton proper, Brian checked up and waved her on. The gesture confused her at first, then broke her heart. He understood she would get problems if mods saw her riding with a rocker boy, so he was letting her go ahead alone. Or maybe it was the other way around. They could work together in solitude, but he couldn't be seen with a mod bird.

She waved back, then headed straight to the Town Hall police station.

The constable assigned to her interview was Officer Carmichael, the copper who beat up Jimmy.

He was an unhappy man, sitting at a paper-strewn desk littered with cigar butts and used teacups. A black telephone sat on the desk corner, papers and reports spilled over the rest. He glanced at the wall clock as she sat down. His wooden seat gave a complaint as he leaned back. "Let's get on with it then, shall we?" he said.

"I apologize for the time. I'm hungry, too."

"You're here for the big mod boy? If so, you'll be too late. Heard we just let the lot of them free on fines. Too early if you ask me, though I guess the constabulary can make do with a few extra quid."

Linda hesitated. She hadn't thought of where the boys' fines would go.

"No, sir," she said, regaining her focus. "I'm here to report a dead boy."

The words stiffened Carmichael. He picked up a pencil. "Tell on?"

Linda explained the situation, leaving Brian out as she'd promised. She was going to tell Carmichael about the glove, but at the last moment she decided against that, too. She didn't know what actually happened on the cliff. Didn't even know if Jimmy and Peter had been there at the same time. She'd been thinking about that as she and Brian had rolled toward town, but only as she watched Carmichael glancing at the clock and as she recalled the casual indifference of both the Saltdean police and the reporter did she see how dangerous giving this piece of information to the police might be.

All of *them* lived in a world where simply keeping the peace was the whole point.

Which meant none of them cared for the truth if it didn't align with that.

"So you don't really know he's dead?" Carmichael asked.

"He went up to the cliffs and didn't come down," Linda said, but it wouldn't have mattered if she'd just confessed out loud because Carmichael kept rambling about endless cases of missing kids and how they all turned up later, usually soused or with split lips from fighting, or high on "the stuff." Kids these days don't have a proper understanding of responsibility, he said, or the common decency to look out for people around them. They don't care for anything but their music and their hair done up like dandies.

His railings made her sufficiently aware of her blouse and her scarf and the purple hearts she'd stuffed into a nook of her handbag.

"So you're not investigating?" she said as he took a breath.

Carmichael wheezed and put his notes markedly at the bottom of a big pile of papers. "Don't you worry, missy," he said, his lips curled in what he might have thought looked like a fatherly smile, but was really just a crystal-clear fahkoff grimace. "We'll get to it when we have the time."

"I see."

He reached over and patted the back of her hand.

"I'm sure your friend will show up tonight and you'll all have a great laugh."

"Yes," she said as she stood up. "I'm sure that's what will happen."

It was edging to full darkness when she stepped out of the station.

She'd parked Jimmy's scooter alongside the road and around the corner. When she got there, Jimmy was fumbling to straddle the seat and failing miserably to kick the starter.

"Hey," she said.

Jimmy looked up. He was ragged now. Bruised and bloodied and clearly without sleep for too long. His eyes looked like punching bags.

"What happened in Saltdean?" Linda asked. They were alone on the street, but the question came out quiet anyway, cold and flat.

Jimmy squinted in the darkening evening.

"Don't lie to me, Jimmy," she said. "I went to the cliffs. I found your glove."

The Lambretta's suspension squeaked as he slumped onto the seat. "I knew Peter was meeting someone," he finally said. "So I went there, too. It was late. He was with the other guy."

"The greaser?"

Jimmy shook his head. "A mod, but he wasn't from around here. They were sitting up there together like nothing."

His answer made her oddly happy because it meant she could trust Brian, that what they had shared on the bluff had been real.

"It made you angry?" she said.

Jimmy crossed his arms on the handlebar and put his forehead on them. When he finally spoke his voice came out hollow. "Why didn't Peter like me?"

"You killed them?"

"No!" He stood up, and almost fell. "I didn't ... I swear I didn't."

"But they're dead."

"It was dark. I scared them."

Linda nodded. It made sense. They'd both probably been taking something—for Peter it would have been dexies—Barry had probably sprung one way and fallen first, Peter had probably run forward. It would have been pitch black. The ground would have been slick with dew.

"I told him not to let go," Jimmy's voice came strained and low. "Don't let go, Peter, I said. Don't you let go." Then Jimmy was crying again, his voice breaking.

Linda understood.

She saw the dug-in boot scar and the bent-down brush.

"You had him," she said.

"He slipped." Jimmy swallowed hard. "Jesus God, he just slipped. I swear it. He just ..."

Linda closed her eyes and put her head back. The glove had come off. Gotten lodged down the cliff while Peter had fallen.

A terrible accident.

"You can't tell anyone," Jimmy said. "Not anyone. They'll kill me, you know they will."

Linda remembered Constable Carmichael's voice as he railed against the youth around him, saw the set of his jaw as he took the expedient path over the truth. That was how the world worked, wasn't it? Make a fuss and pay a price. Keep the row and things will happen for you. It was her father's world, anyway. And in this case, she understood exactly what was at stake for Jimmy Smith.

She wanted to do what was right, but what was right?

Tell the truth and leave Jimmy to the whims of the constables and the rest of a society who invalidated the worlds he lived in, or lie and leave Peter's story ... unfinished.

Jimmy drew a wracking breath.

Whatever her choice, Jimmy Smith was going to pay for what happened last night for the rest of his life.

She was too tired to take this on now. Too tired and too angry.

She pushed Jimmy back in the seat, then slid on in front. "Looks like you need a ride home," she said.

When she kicked the Lambretta on, the strength of the engine made her think of Brian.

Where was he now? With his rocker gang? With another boy? Maybe he was one who went both ways—so maybe he was with another girl. Or maybe he'd just gone home. Maybe he was disappearing into an Elvis record like she did with the Eyes.

Were they that different?

"Hold tight," she said.

Jimmy wrapped his arms around her, and she drove him home.

Monday morning she stepped into the offices of the *Daily News*.

She wore a print blouse with brilliant yellow and black bands under a perfectly tailored suit jacket. The necklace was polished sea glass that changed its tone of green depending on the light. Her hair was perfect, her mascara thicker than usual. Her skirt was a comfortable black piece from Dabney's, a super little shop north of town where the seamstress did her own work. It cut across the top of her knees and showed a scandalous amount of skin, but the pull of it across her legs as she walked made her feel sharp. The boots were the pair she'd gotten with Pamela, and they brought the whole thing together in a way that felt bold and strong.

She pulled a pair of dark glasses from her eyes.

It had taken a never-ending pot of coffee and the entire night, but the weight of the package jutting from her handbag meant it had been worth it.

"Are you all right, Linda?" said Mercedes Kent, Mr. Deitz's young secretary. Mercedes' father and Deitz were schooltime pals, though that hadn't kept Mr. Deitz from having wandering eyes and likely wandering hands. He'd tried it with Linda a few times, and she'd needed the job enough that she'd put up with it. But then, she'd put up with a lot of things before.

"I'm fine," she replied as she walked into Deitz's office.

He looked up, readers perched on his nose.

She smiled, lifted her manuscript, and dropped it on his desk with a thud that raised dust.

The title stood out on the page.

Us vs. Them.

Deitz lifted the title page and scanned the next.

Some of what follows here actually happened. Some of it I made up. But when you read it, you'll know all of it is true.

"What is this?" Mr. Deitz said.

"It's my story."

"It was supposed to be about Mame's Boutique."

"Oh, it's in there," she said.

"You know I can't use this, right?"

Linda did her best impression of Constable Carmichael's expression last evening. "No, I suppose you can't."

She plucked the manuscript back.

"Go and do me a real story or you'll not be getting paid. And if we have to cover dress code again, you'll not be keeping your job."

"That's fine, Mr. Deitz," she said as she stuffed the pages back into her handbag. "I've come across another paper that wants to run it, and their dress code is a much better fit."

"Who would run that rubbish?"

She ignored his question, turning instead on her totally fab heel and stepping out the door, through the lobby, and into the morning air.

There were stories to be written today, dozens of them.

And Linda Brennan, editor of Britain's freshest independent culture page, was going to write her share.

Ron's Foreword: _"Prospecting"_

"Prospecting" was originally created for the _Fiction River: Justice_ volume, but found its home instead in _Fiction River: Hard Choices,_ which was edited by Dean Wesley Smith, and where, to be honest, it makes more sense. Sometimes the just world does that, you know?

The story itself represents my first attempt at writing a "western," and springs from a bit of history that I'd learned a while back and made me step back to see things quite a bit differently.

Prospecting

The gent was broke down, his wagon done stuck in a wash full of Juneberry and brush, listing to the front and north as it heads west. It's a simple wagon, floor slats weathered but not gone to silver, rails on both sides. He's got the bed covered with a tarp, and a healthy enough mule standing a'front of it.

I'm two days from Yreka, a mining town in the northern territory of California that you pronounce "Why-reeka," like it's a question rather than a place. It's mid-morning time, so the coyotes ain't up and yapping, and the mountain lions probably won't be willing to make a go of it for now. The air's fresh and clear, nothing in the sky but a few wisps of cloud and a dark pair of eagle-hawks up hunting rabbits. It ain't rained for a week, so all's a body can smell is the rock baking in the sun and the coyote brush that's growing out of cracks in that same rock.

The fella's a city gent, though. No doubt about that.

Oh, he's dirty enough, and his skin's got the roughness that comes from being on the trail a fetch. But I know he's city folk by the fact he don't put his iron in his hand as I come up to help him. Any man that's been around the mountains long enough knows better than to trust another man out here, don't matter that he's white or not. They ain't all like me. Some folk here got no scruples. But this gent leaves his rifle propped against the wagon bed even as he sees me standing up here with my own rifle pointed down from my hip, so I get right away that he's a city man.

"You all right?" I tell him as I come down the ridge.

The trigger guard on his gun gleams in the early sun.

The gent turns out to be a kid. Could be maybe twenty years old, or could be maybe less. He's sweating through a shirt that's scruffed up with dust from at least as far back as Kansas and Missouri territory, probably on farther. His black hair's matted down in the heat, and his mustache is dark enough to stand up against a couple day's beard. He's a bit of a Nancy boy, too: hang-dog thin in the jaw, the kind of thin that the womenfolk would take more than easy to if there was any womenfolk to be found around these parts.

I figure him for a Wop.

Maybe his daddy come over from the boot.

I got no trouble with Wops, mind you. I done worked with all kinds in my life, and I figure one man's as good or bad as another.

"The wheel's busted," he says, standing taller as I come up close. "Can't get the son of a bitch off."

"Mind if I take a look," I tell him.

He nods and I come up to the wagon, then push my hat up my forehead.

"Wheel's busted up all right," I say.

"Axle's good and bent, too," he replies.

"I ain't no wheelwright," I say, "but the spoke looks like it's still good. Gonna take some working to get you heading on all right, but I think it'll stand a patching."

"Yeah. If I can get it off to begin with, anyway."

He wipes the sleeve of his shirt over his brow and shields his gaze from the sun.

"Brighter up here than you're used to, ain't it?" I say.

"A little."

"Best get used to it. California territory's probably a different place in a lotta ways."

"Probably."

"Where you from?" I ask.

"Pennsylvania," he says. "Philadelphia."

"Ah. The Keystone state."

"That's right."

"Kip," I say as I hold out my hand.

"Lonzo," he replies. "Lonzo Bassi."

I nod. Definitely a Wop.

I set my own gun down and lift on the wagon's edge while Lonzo knocks the hub ring over and gets the wheel off. "I'll have to get the band put back on when I get to a town," he says as he brings a big rock over to put under the axle strut so I can lay it on down again.

"Yeah. That'd be good."

I straighten my back and pull my skin out to take a slug of water.

"That's a load off," I say.

"Much appreciated," Lonzo replies.

I sit on a rock and gnaw on some dried steer I bought while I was in Yreka, and I watch as he goes about pounding the axle straight and then nailing a pair of slats up against the wheel that'll keep it in the round well enough to spin all right. The kid was handier than he looked—then again, I s'pose if he wasn't, the Blackfoot or the Sioux would've probably kilt him on the way out here, so sometimes the good Lord's world does make a lick of sense.

"What are you doing out here?" he says when he's done with the wheel. "Prospecting?"

I grin over at him, and I spit a piece of leather. "Ain't we all?"

He smiles back and I see that same gleam that rides on the gazes of pretty much every gent who's been streaming into California for the past couple years. The boy's here to make his fortune.

"Heading to your claim?" he asks.

I chuckle at him. "Wouldn't you like to know?"

Lonzo grins like a man's been caught holding an ace high. "I hear you can pick the gold up straight off the ground out around San Francisco," he says.

"Maybe a while back."

"What do you mean?"

I ignore the question. This ain't 1849 no more. If the stupid Wop didn't already know that all the easy gold was long gone, I wasn't scheming to be the one that breaks it to him.

"You're a shade north if you're looking for Frisco," I say.

"Figured I would be. Worth it to get past the Sierra Nevada, though."

"That makes sense."

"How far north?" he asks.

"Hundred mile. Maybe a little more."

Lonzo sighs and rolls the wheel over next to the wagon.

"How can I repay you?" he says when we get it back on right again.

"Well," I tell him, "I got some business up north 'round the lake. If you're willing to take a detour, I might be obliged to hitch a ride rather than walk it."

"How far is it?"

"Not more 'n half a day. With the wagon, we probably get there by sundown tonight."

He shrugs and puts his hat on. "I've been on the road four months already. Another day can't hurt me none."

"Much obliged," I say.

"So," Lonzo says as the wagon jolts its way over the high plains. "Just how does a man go about making his claim here?"

We're headed north-ways. It's all rock and brush behind us, with low mountains rising up ahead and to the west, and with the hint of the Sierra Nevada down to the south and east where Lonzo done come from. Mule's making good time, and the sun's edging on past its peak.

"Simple enough," I say.

He waits.

"You just find a plot big enough you think you can handle it all without no help, and you mark it out."

"That's it?"

"Pretty much. Course, you got to keep working it. You leave a claim fallow for any real time and another gent might jump it."

Lonzo smirked at that. "Maybe I do it the easy way and just jump *your* claim?"

"Don't joke. There be men who'll do that."

"Maybe I'm one of them."

I look at him, sitting on the driver's seat, sweating and grinning. Does this city Yankee actually got it in him to jump a claim? He seems soft, but I know sometimes it's the soft ones you need to keep your watch out after.

"I don't think you are," I finally decide. "Besides, I doubt you got any interest in my place."

"Dangerous site?"

"Let's just say I ain't worried."

We get quiet for a bit.

"That's a nice gun you got over there," I finally say as we roll over a hillside.

Lonzo's got his rifle placed into a holster he's built into the side of the wagon.

"Thank you, much," he says. "It's a Sharps. Breech loader."

"Ain't never seen one like it."

"I'd be surprised if you did. It's a new one. Made in Philly." He jangles something in his pant pocket. "Takes a cartridge, which means I can reload in a couple seconds flat."

"Sumbitch," I say. "Shoot pretty good?"

Lonzo purses his lips and squints up toward the mountain ridge off to the east. "I reckon I can pick a bird off at eleven hundred yards with it."

I chuff at that.

"I don't expect no Yankee can shoot that good no matter what the rifle."

"My daddy taught me."

I contemplate that. Maybe there's something more to Lonzo than meets the eye.

"Eleven hundred yards," I say. "That's pretty good, then."

I don't need to tell him mine's just an old Mississippi rifle, a muzzle loader probably ten years old if it's a day. It may be showing age, but we get 'long just fine together, and it's saved my behind more than a few times. Regardless what the Wop thinks of my rifle, I figure he got no need to know about the Colt I carry in my pack, 'long with 'bout everything else I own.

The road's bumpy, but it still beats walking. The mule's doing just fine all by itself.

"Where *you* from?" Lonzo asks after a bit.

"Oh, all over."

"Where abouts is All Over?"

I look across at him and decide it's just an honest question from an honest man. Probably can't hurt none to be sociable. He done told me about being from Philly, after all.

"Started in Rockingham County, North Carolina," I say. "Daddy was a shoe man by trade, though my mama called him more a gambler and a drinker by temperament. He done run off by hisself when I was a boy, though, so I don't recall him much."

"Poor woman."

I shift around on the seat, and see a coyote come up along the ridge, then another. No surprise there, as a coyote travels in twos when it kin.

"Mangy things," Lonzo says. "Maybe I get a chance to show you the Sharps in action?"

"Shouldn't be no problem," I tell him back. "A coyote's not going to hurt you none, less you happen to be a rabbit or less you fall into a den of their younglin's. A wolf's different thing, though. A pack a wolves'll bring a man down if you give 'em a chance. See a wolf and you're best off to shoot him straight out."

Lonzo don't seem convinced, but he leaves his rifle in its place.

The wagon rolls on, and pretty soon the coyotes leave us to ourselves.

"What about your mama?" Lonzo finally says.

"What about her?"

"You said your daddy was a cobbler. What about your mama?"

"Well, she did some looming at a cotton farm for a bit, and she'd sell pies she baked." I scoff. "Least she'd sell the ones I didn't eat up first."

Lonzo laughs the right amount.

"Worst whippin' I ever got was for eating a rhubarb pie she already tabbed for the manor man." I stop my yapping to remember that night: hadn't thought about it in a while. "I can still hear the sound of that switch falling and recall how I was wondering if that was what the nigger boys felt when they got their whippin's."

Lonzo gives pause when he hears me talking 'bout the whippings, just long enough that I ponder if I got me a Yankee gent here with an abolitional streak in him, but he don't say nothing else about it and just goes on.

"Sounds like a good woman," he says.

"Probably," I say. "She done her best anyway, and I s'pose I come out okay in the end."

Lonzo nods.

"Left home after that and went to working at a tobacco farm so I could eat."

I ain't done this much talking since I come to California, but Lonzo's got his questions and he's listening, and the ground is rolling by just fine. The more I spin tales, the easier they come. I tell him a story about hopping a rail car west toward Tennessee, and fixing the roof of a man's house for five dollars one time.

"Then I got up north your way," I say.

"Pennsylvania?"

"Yep. Worked the rails in Philly for a bit."

"You don't say? Wonder if we might have met before?"

I shake my head. "Not likely," I say. "Not less you mixed it up with the Micks any. That's where I stayed most the time I was there. They's the ones done all the real work on the rails up in Philly. Come off the boat spiking and drinking, they did. Not the brightest of folk, I s'pose, but not a one of 'em was afeared of a day's work and they were all good in a fight."

"That's probably fair enough description," Lonzo says. "Some of the Irish came to my father's restaurant."

"Restaurant?"

"My family is into food."

I smirk at him. Dad's a cook. Maybe that's where he gets his soft from.

"That what you got in back?" I say. "Pots 'n pans?"

"No. Not really. Well, some pots and pans. But mostly I got my tent and my tools to mine with back there, though I'll rightly fess up to being able to rustle you a tasty plate of rabbit if you'll give me the time."

He peels back the tarp.

True fact, there's a tent kit back there and tools and utensils. He's got hisself a boxy suitcase that stores, I assume, all his other grimy shirts and pants.

I cluck my understanding of what I see, and he drops the tarp.

"Anyway," I say, picking up on my story. "That's where I spent most of my time when I was there in Philly—driving rail ties with the Micks and the Polacks. Weren't there very long, though."

"Why'd you leave?"

I think about how the city was so blamed crowded with people wanting nothing more than to tell a man what to do and when to do it, and how the buildings were so dirty and stacked up atop one another like bricks. The memory alone makes me pucker up.

"Don't think I'm cut out to be a Yankee."

Lonzo looks at me. "Probably not."

"You planning to head on back there once you get all riched up?" I say.

"Suppose I will," Lonzo replies.

I just smile.

I seen it a few times before: a prim, young dandy gent comes strolling themselves into California territory as if they own the place, thinking to spend a few months out here before cartin' back a wagonload of gold. A few make it back rich like that— enough that the word gets out, anyway, and enough that a hundred more gleamy-eyed bastards like Lonzo come following along for every one that makes it.

Problem is, the world works its own way, and that way ain't always so kind to the second man out. The early bird gets the worm, and all.

"What'd you do when you left Philly?" he asks me.

"Drifted west. Did some trapping and trading till those got

tapped out, then some river boating. Finally found myself in St. Louis with that outfit working to drive the rails out to California. Worked that job 'till one day I decided I couldn't handle the foreman's sass no more. Bought me a gun and a bottle that night, and just headed west. Ain't looked back since."

"I see I'm with a world traveler," Lonzo says.

"Don't know about that," I reply. "But I'll allow as to wishing I had that bottle with me right about now."

We both laugh.

The mule makes better time than I expect, but still the sunlight's fading as we come up to the pass, and climb our way to where we see down into the lakebed valley.

The clouds above are catching the last rays and turning the sky into a bright orange fire with red and purple flares, and the valley mountains are turning their own colors, dark and light, gold and purple, sharp on the edges like God hisself done drawn 'em there. The lake water is the brightest blue there is, and it's rippled with waves that spread out north toward Mt. Shasta on straight ahead, the peak white-tipped even in the month of August. That place points itself up toward where the Heavens lay, and it makes the dry ledges and crests around us seem like they ain't nothing but young pups.

That's what I like about it out here, you know?

Mountains like this make a man understand what being free means.

They give a man to do what he wants. No bosses haranguing over him, no coppers running around telling him where he can sleep and where he can't sleep. A man gets to live out here like the good Lord promised he could.

"Think we should make camp?" Lonzo says. "Maybe down by the water?"

I got eyes for something else, though—something I been looking for in the first place: a scattering of three thatched tule huts and a taut-set teepee built along a line that's half rocks and half trees. There's a thin smoke from cook fire.

Modoc Indians—just like the miners I heard tell back in Yreka said they'd be.

Lonzo sees what I'm looking at, too.

"What should we do?" he says.

I slide out the seat, and my boots hit the ground with a rocky crunch.

"Give me your gun," I say.

"What?"

"I said give me your gun, and I'll handle this."

"I ain't giving you my weapon," he says.

I reach around my pack and grab the Colt out of it, then I point it up at the kid.

Lonzo, to his credit, freezes, then raises his hands up slow-like.

"Don't be a cussed fool, now, Lonzo," I say. "Give me your gun, and I'll handle this."

Lonzo reaches the rifle up and gives it over my way.

"Loaded?" I ask.

"Of course."

"Bullets?"

He reaches into a pocket and hands over a pouch. It's nice and weighty. I loop it onto my belt, and drop the Colt back into the pack.

"Go on and get a fire going," I say as I turn toward the Indians. "I'll be back in a bit. Maybe have some of that rabbit you were bragging on so high."

"What are you going to do?"

"Just what I said I was."

I walk away, then.

My legs are stiff from setting too long, so it feels good to move.

The clearing's full of sawgrass that comes up past my knees. I hear birds from far off, and catch the reek of fresh droppings close by. My boots crunch over the ground as I draw up closer to the Indian shelters. I got my Mississippi rifle in one hand and Lonzo's newfangled gun in the other. I look the Sharps over as I walk along, seeing how the loader works. The cartridges rattle against my thigh, and the Colt is hard and heavy at the small of my back.

Four shelters.

Probably no more than twelve or fifteen Modoc, several probably young.

They don't see me yet, but three of 'em are in the open: a squaw's standing by one of the huts, and two others are carrying lines of fish as they come up from the lakeside.

I use my own gun to shoot the squaw.

She falls over and don't move again.

I drop that rifle and grab the other. We'll see whether Lonzo was lying about it now.

It feels different against my shoulder, but it ain't long afore the next shot rings out and one of the fishing Indians drops. I fetch a new cartridge from the pouch and pop open the breech. Less than five counts later I got a bead on Indian number three and I press the shot off to great success.

Hell of a weapon.

I reload again as I walk through the sawgrass, thinking that next town I get to will mean steak and adventurous womenfolk for a week.

Another Indian comes from inside a hut.

I shoot her and reload so fast that echoes from the rifle are still ringing in the valley as I'm ready to shoot again. A few steps later I get the fifth—a male this time. Now they're running, three of 'em anyway. Seeing as I know how to hunt, it won't matter none. There's a ring of rocks at the edge of the campground that I know the younglin's make in their play. Two come out the teepee. I shoot the one that's got a gun, and the other runs off down the lakebed as I take a moment to reload.

Always hate to shoot a younglin' cause they pay so well alive.

Their fire smells of fir.

The first hut is empty now. The second has two younglin's in it, huddling down in a woolen blanket.

Helluva day, I think. It's one helluva day.

I straighten up, looking after the runners.

A shot cracks out, and Jesus Mother Mary, it's like I get kicked in the back of the shoulder.

I spin round and hit the ground on my side.

It's like I can't breathe for a long many seconds.

I lay there with my cheek pressed against the dirt. My vision waters up and I got to blink, but I still can't take in a breath.

The two Indian whelps look at me through the entryway to that thatched-up hut that's nearly going to rot. Their eyes are big and white. For a minute I see a memory of my brother, Jess and me, hiding in the cold cellar while Daddy got to arguing with Mama. I bet our eyes were like that. I bet these kids are pissing their little britches about right now.

Then a breath finally comes, and the pain hits like fire.

"I been shot," I say to the Indians.

I must have missed a Modoc in my earlier accounting. One of them must have been coming along behind. Maybe hunting. Must have had a rifle out on his own.

Blam'd stupid. Should have paid it better mind.

I blink away the waves of tears that gum up my eyesight.

Lonzo's rifle is tossed in the dirt across the way where I flung it as I dropped.

Got to get it back before the Modoc comes along to finish the job.

I take my good arm and crawl toward it, but the fire in the other shoulder's like a knife twisting in, and I can't move on account of the need to catch my breath again.

Footsteps come along and I know I ain't getting to the Sharps in time.

I reach back with my good hand into my pack and get my grips around the Colt, then I twist around and look up.

Rather than an Indian's face, I see Lonzo instead. He's standing at the edge of the campground, breathing heavy like he's been running.

"Thank God," I say as I lay back. "I almost shot ya."

"What in the nine hells are you doing!" he screams at me.

Then I see he's got my rifle gripped in his hands, his knuckles are nearly as pure and white as his face. The truth hits like a river current.

"It's you that shot me?" I say, turning the Colt back on him. "Now why'd you go and do all that?"

"You're killing them!"

"Of course I'm killing 'em."

I wave my Colt at him again.

I want to shoot the son of a bitch right where he stands, but I figure my shoulder's tore up pretty good. The blood's flowing wet anyways, and I feel the lead up high in my chest. I'm finding regular breath now, though, and I can sit up all right, so that's what I do. I groan and I grunt, but I get myself to a place where I can look at Lonzo like a man.

Maybe I'll make it through this all right.

"How about you help get me patched up like you done that wheel of yours?" I say. "That'll give you time to argue the case of why I shouldn't just shoot you right now and have it over with."

Lonzo grips the rifle harder and glances to his own gun there in the dirt. There's a calculating going on inside his mind. We both know he can't load up that rifle of mine again before I plug him full of this gun—just like we both know he can't get to his own gun no faster.

"Get yourself calmed down, Lonzo," I say. "This ain't nothing to get shot over."

"You can't go killing people like that, Kip."

"Sure I can. They's just Indians. And by my accounting *these* Indians just made me thirty dollars, plus whatever I can get for the younglin's at the courthouse."

"Thirty dollars?"

"I ain't got the time to talk 'bout this if you ain't fixing my shoulder."

I aim at his forehead, and figure he knows I'll hit it.

Lonzo finally lays the weapon on down. His gaze flickers over to the dead squaw, though, so I see he's not fully on board with me yet, but he does come over to look at my shoulder. I got a moment to sway him.

"Indians bring good money, Lonzo. You best learn that now. Five dollars gold for every dead one, and whatever someone'll pay for the orphan-kids."

He pulls the shirt off the bullet hole. Stings like a hive of hornets digging into my back.

"I thought you were a prospector?" he says.

I gather my breath before answering.

"You prospect for gold, I go looking for Indians. I figure it for the same thing, except the land's going to be running dry of gold a long time before it runs out of Indians."

I feel the knife on my throat before I hear nothing.

He must have had it in his boot.

"Put the gun down, Kip," he says.

"Don't get too smart for those britches, boy," I reply. "Think hard over what you're getting ready to do before you do it."

"I swear to the man above, I'm going to take you to the sheriff."

I laugh and it hurts down my back and into my chest. The Colt's still in my hand, and I know I can lift it up to shoot him, but I ain't sure of the timing of it all. I figure Lonzo's probably okay with a knife, but I ain't sure if he'll butcher me right out here in the open air or not.

"Go on and take me to the sheriff," I say once I get myself under control. "He's the one layin' the gold."

"That's bull," Lonzo said. "No lawman worth his badge would run a bounty."

"Well, teck-nickly it'd be the judge at the courthouse paying on the younglins. He's the one got to rule if they's orphans or not—which I figure he'll see it as such since I done shot the mamas and the papas."

"I don't understand you at all."

"Don't go straining your head too far, Lonzo. This is just how it is out here in this territory. I can't say at all how much gold the good Lord done put in the ground around these parts, but I *can* tell you that the good state of California done promised to pay up in that gold for every dead Indian a man can get his hands on, and they been making good on that word for a year now."

"The *state* is paying you to hunt Indians?"

"Five dollars a head. Payable at the jailhouse."

The knife presses harder and I'm feeling a burn.

"Plus expenses," I add on. I get my finger ready on the trigger because, no matter what Lonzo decides, I ain't planning on dying out here alone. "So, you feel free to take me on up to the next judge you can find. I can recommend Yreka just a couple days back, and French Gulch ain't much farther if you prefer taking a more southerly way. But right now I need you get to fishing out that bullet you done put in my back."

"That's not right," he says in a voice that's like he's talking mostly to himself. "That can't be right."

The knife comes off my neck, though.

I turn round and shoot him square in the forehead. He falls back near the hut.

Sumbitch.

He brung it on hisself, but still it bothers the hell out of me.

I never shot a white man before, and I ain't sure what to do about that.

I leave the Modoc where they all lay.

Lonzo, too.

I may not be the sharpest steel trap 'round, but I know I ain't got the time to go collecting up dead Indians now. I'm setting to die if I don't get me some help soon. The mule wagon can make Yreka in a day at best, maybe. If I make it to town, I can come back later and see what the crows and the coyotes done left for me.

After thinking on it bit, I decide leaving Lonzo out here don't bother me none at all, though. Turns out a Yankee's worth less than an Indian.

Standing hurts, but I can do it.

Walking ain't no different.

I hold onto the Colt as I go, and it gives me a feeling of no little strength.

It's getting to be almost dark when I come to the mule and the wagon. I barely got strength enough to slide up to the seat and hit the mule to get it to walking.

The blood's not good. Too much, sluicing all over the seat.

I'm draining too fast and I'm losing my thoughts in the darkness. The coyotes begin their yips as I get under Lonzo's tarp and begin looking for a needle and thread to work on myself as best I kin. Dandy Yankee cook ought to have something like that, oughtn't he?

I crack open the suitcase.

It's too dark to see in, so I dump it over.

Can't feel my fingers now.

I need to rest a bit, but the wagon's already stopped its bumping and thumping.

Dumbass mule.

"Get up!" I yell at it, too weak to do much more. "Get up!"

But the mule don't move.

I'm sitting here, alone in the back of a dead man's wagon.

Over in the dark distance I see still the outline of three huts and a teepee. Can't see Lonzo or the Indians, but I'm thinking I see the younglins moving.

"Hey!" I yell out. "Come here! Come here!"

That's when I see the wolf.

It's a big-chested monster standing on the ridge with its dark fur ruffled up along the back of his neck. Its nostrils flare with that sense it gets when an animal smells blood. Its eyes are cold and black.

The Colt is heavier than it was earlier, but I get it up to aim. My shot goes too high, and the gun kicks itself away and claps itself down to the ground.

The sound of the shot scares the mule, though, and the wagon bounces along for a ways.

A minute later, or is it an hour, I see the wolves again.

It's getting' dark but that won't stop them none.

The huntin' pack is forming up, coming along to make a meal of the mule at the front of the wagon and the man at the back. I got no gun now. I got no gun, and the wolves they keep coming.

I think of when my daddy went to wailing on my mama, and I remember the beatings I got when the boss man didn't like me talking back. I think of the money I got left lying on the ground out by the lakebed.

That's not right, I hear Lonzo say.

I look up into the sky and see the stars shining there in the way they been shining since the good Lord hisself put them up there.

"Day of the Party" is arguably the first piece I ever wrote, back many years ago when I decided I wanted to get serious about becoming a real writer. I was on assignment in Washington, D.C. and had lots of time on my hands. I'd always wanted to write, and I figured why not, right? To be clear, the piece I wrote then bears perhaps only a passing resemblance to what you'll see here. That's because when Kris Rusch said she wanted stories for *Fiction River: Broken Dreams*, I pulled it out, and with a few years of experience under my belt, saw now where it had gone off the rails. Proof that there are no bad ideas, only bad execution? You tell me.

That said, I should also note that this story—even in its initial state—was always my mother's very favorite story of mine. She cried the first time she read it. So in whatever form, I'll never be able to think of it without seeing her. Which is another reason that it, too, is one of my own favorites.

Day of the Party

Having spent a restless night of brief sleeps, she woke early.

The sheets rustled as the woman slid out of bed, her husband still lying on his back and gently snoring. He, too, had been feigning sleep through most of the night, so it was no surprise he slept late.

Sitting on the edge of the bed, she put her toes into a worn pair of corded slippers and, thinking of Bill, looked out the window.

For a minute her son's arms were around her shoulders and the clothy aroma of the jacket he was wearing the last time she saw him expanded to fill her body. The sensation was like warm wool pressed against everything inside her: her ribs, her lungs, her arms and fingers. It raised heat under her cheeks, and layered a coarse taste across the lining of her tongue. She felt it in every strand of her hair, against her lungs as she took in a breath, and down under her skin as she exhaled. Her toes tingled inside her slippers. Then, as it always did, everything faded to leave just the morning sky with its dull shade of overcast, a shade that matched the gray in her hair and that was tinged with the faint aroma of the ocean a distance away.

The mist clinging to the window obscured the dogwoods out back as if it wanted to bring a stop to the day.

She wouldn't have argued if it had won its case.

Despite herself, she would be fine if time could have just halted right here.

Forty-five years, she thought as she rose from the bed.

Forty-five.

Her routine happened without conscious thought—coffee machine filled, newspaper retrieved from the mailbox, thin slices of wheat bread inserted into the two farthest right slots of the toaster. It was a process executed with the precision of years of practice.

Wrapping cold fingers around the heat of her mug, she stepped into the glass-encased patio deck and sat down to eat. She spread the paper beside her, using the seat of the glider as a table. She knew how to use the Internet and even surprised both her husband and her great-grandkids by creating an Instagram account a couple months ago, but it was her usual practice to scan the headlines and read the local section. She wasn't going to change that now. Today, though, she let the pages sit there and just stared into the morning mist with a gaze that had no focus.

She remained like that, motionless save the gentle sway of the glider, as her coffee grew cold and the toast became stale.

She decided to walk to the grocery.

It took several minutes longer than driving, but the exercise was good. Though she was eighty-one, she was still vigorous and didn't want to lose that. She was, however, also old enough to know better than to tell herself lies. The opportunity for extra time alone also had something to do with her choice of going on foot.

The smell of cut flowers and fresh produce greeted her as she entered the store.

She gave the grocer a comfortable, closed-lipped grin.

With few exceptions, they had been greeting each other like that every day for a very long time. She picked out food for the guests—cold cuts, chips, and other snack food—all the standards.

As they did every year, she and her husband would be hosting young Bill's birthday party this afternoon. He had been her first great-grandchild, and was named after her own Bill. At first she didn't know how to feel about using a name that would always remind her of her boy, but she also knew it was appropriate. The boy was Bill's grandson, after all. Like everything else that happened after they received the visit and the flag, though, the idea of young Bill carrying her boy's name was filled with conflict.

The young man would be thirteen years old today.

Time flies, the small voice inside her head said at one point. *I can't believe it's been that long*. It was a lie, of course. But this time it was a good lie, so she let it remain in her mind without further remark.

The grocer made small talk as he rang up the bill. His son had just taken a new job with a contractor who was building the new library on campus. His daughter was getting ready to start another semester at UM. Go Terps, he said. Go Terps, she replied. Emmie had graduated from there a few years back. She expected young Bill would be attending in a few more.

She paid and started to leave, but the man touched her on the sleeve and placed another small package into her bag. A chocolate bar.

"It's for Bill," he explained.

She smiled. "Thank you," she said.

On the way home she stopped at the gift shop and bought a roll of colored ribbon.

It wouldn't do to have a party without some decoration.

She dabbed on the last of her lipstick and pulled at the hang of her dress, frowning at the way time has of making clothes fit differently than you're used to. Peering into the mirror she saw a few strands of silver hair had slipped the bonds of their tortoiseshell restraint. The delicate band was a bit out of style for someone of her age, but her Bill had given it to her when he was just a boy and she had worn it every year since then. She didn't care if it was too young for her now. A moment later the renegade hairs were reined in and the rest smoothed out.

The morning fog had given way to a bright day.

She had time for one more pass through the house before the family arrived.

Outside, her husband stoked the grill in preparation for the feast that all but she would enjoy.

It would be all right, though. She had difficulty eating at these parties, but the crowded atmosphere meant it was never too hard to avoid scrutiny. That was one reason she liked holding this party every year. It was easier to hide in a crowd than it was when they were alone.

Her husband, too, was getting old.

His middle had expanded and the lines in his face had gotten deeper. She rarely saw those lines, though. This surprised her, actually. She had to look hard to see the lines that ran down his cheeks and around his lips because, when she looked at him, the man she saw was still the shy boy who followed her home from school for a week before asking her out.

She watched him prod the coals with casual intention, remembering their last honeymoon, a two-week cruise to Hawaii that his company had given him when he finally retired. For a minute she recalled pineapple and flowers and the salt of the sea. She thought about Waikiki and volcanoes, emerald water and their tour of Pearl Harbor. She remembered the way her heart clenched at the sight of shards of the *Arizona* as they rose from the shallows, and the way her husband had guided her away when he realized what she was thinking, the way they sat there on the boardwalk later that night, silently, just holding hands and breathing in the salted air.

If anything, she thought as her husband straightened from the grill, he had grown more handsome as time passed.

A car door slammed out front.

Her daughter and son-in-law called from the front yard.

She straightened the drape.

It would be okay, she thought as she left the window. Everything would be okay.

The party was a rousing success by every standard.

Her husband brought howls of delight from the men when he destroyed the first batch of burgers, but the barbecue had been wonderful anyway.

The house rang with sounds of youthful exuberance—a wide range of grandchildren and great-grandchildren playing hide-and-seek and whatever other games they came up with, screaming in shrill voices as they streaked to the safety of home bases or until their parents finally put an end to it.

Bill, of course, had gotten his share of attention as the birthday boy. Their family was large enough to create a constant string of opportunities for get-togethers, but small enough to allow them the cozy touches of hugs and the off-key singing of "Happy Birthday." And, of course, there had been the prerequisite mound of presents that never failed to create jealousy among the children.

And she enjoyed the girl-talk.

Seeing the whole chain of young women in her family always made her happy.

That was something, anyway.

They were each so beautiful. Each in the glory of mid-life, with so much activity surrounding them that they couldn't recognize how much they were actually accomplishing. Emmie was in Finance. Kathy was going back to school for a psychology degree. The elderly woman listened as they complained about work and their kids, and as they joked about the men.

At one point, though, she found herself looking out the window and staring into the sky.

The party was over now.

The house was the exact same quiet as the silence that came over their church after the sermon was over and the people had gone.

They passed a few absentminded minutes cleaning up the mess left behind. She ran a wet rag over the cabinets and table, picking up dried crumbs of chocolate cake. Her husband took large bags of garbage to the streetside, each tied at the top with bright yellow clips. He cleaned the grill and returned it to its proper place in the garage.

"Are you ready to go?" he asked when he came back to the house.

"Yes," she replied. It was time to go, so she was ready.

She picked up a slim purse, the flowers from the grocery, and the brown paper bag.

Her husband stood at the passenger side of their blue sedan, and closed the door after her. She didn't mind getting into the car without his help, but it was something he took pride in so when they parked she again waited as her husband came around and helped her out.

They walked slowly and in silence for several minutes, leaving the garage behind and progressing over the wide sidewalks that lined the stately buildings of the nation's capital.

Across the open plaza, the last rays of the sun colored the sky.

The breeze was fresh and clean, muting the sound of people's voices as they talked in the open air.

A blanket of green grass absorbed the sound of their footsteps, but she heard their walking anyway: their soft breathing that came harder with every year, the rasp of their clothes in movement, the crinkle of the paper bag. She pulled the tortoiseshell band away to let her hair waft on the evening breeze. She didn't react to the brief smile her movement brought to her husband's face, but she noticed.

Finally, as she did every time, she glanced up to the face of Abraham Lincoln gazing out toward the Capitol Building, his chiseled white nose pointed and sharp, his sunken eyes wise but beleaguered. It was a familiar face, she thought. It made her feel something she wished she could explain.

They arrived at the monument.

Its black walls were familiar by now, too, smooth and polished, angling away like polished wings, imposing with all its names.

Again, the weight of her husband's hand on the small of her back directed her to the place. Again, she didn't need the guidance, but took comfort in the fact that it was provided. Kneeling carefully to keep her balance, she placed the grocery bag on the ground and carefully extracted its contents.

The flowers shook in stiff waves as she put the pot in its place, their crimson shoots vivid against the tower of black granite. As always, she nestled a laminated placard amongst the flowers, then she returned to the bag to pull out the block of candy the grocer had put there.

She laid it gently against the wall.

Chocolate had always been Bill's favorite.

Her husband got to one knee beside her. He wrapped his arm tight over her shoulders as the sun fell below the horizon and the cold weight of the wall loomed hard above. The pressure brought back the clothy smell of her boy's jacket from so long ago.

Why, she thought.

Why Vietnam?

Why that hill?

Why had her boy died in a distant land, saving three other boys in his command? Her husband's grip made her remember one of those three boys, the one who found them a few years ago and spent an hour telling her about his family, his kids who lived now because of Bill. He showed her pictures as he cried. She remembered the weight of his forehead on her shoulder, and the way her heart ached for weeks afterward.

There was never going to be an answer.

She knew that now, after all these years.

Or maybe there were a million answers, which was really no different. Freedom. Communism. Duty. Sense of honor. Capitalism, or just a simple draft number.

A million answers meant there was none.

A million answers meant the hole in her life would never heal.

She scanned the dark panel of names, thinking about her boy and thinking about the trail of oil that still drained from a battleship sunk in a different war and a different time.

Beside her, her husband cleared his throat.

He blinked his eyes, and took in a strong breath before speaking.

"They look good," he croaked, nodding at the flowers.

She nodded back, swallowing hard.

Finally, as she did every year, she read the card.

Dearest Bill, she said.

I can scarcely believe it's been forty-five years since the day you were killed. We both miss you as dearly today as we did then, and we wish with all our heart you were here with us.

We will never forget you.

We hosted your grandson's birthday party this year. You would be proud of him. He is so beautiful.

He has your eyes ...

The Ten Days of Newtonmas

On the day of Christmas Eve, Ella's "true love" sent her a link to an online tone generator. It turned out to be more romantic than it sounds, but not by much. He was, after all, a man of physics.

She was sitting in the store's food court, using up the last moments of her precious break to scroll through her phone, when the email arrived.

Merry Newtonmas! it read. *Hope you have fun!*

Then came the link and signature: Benjamin A. Stiles, Dreamy Associate Professor, Belknap College Physics Department.

Newtonmas? What the hell was that?

And, Dreamy?

The answer to the "Dreamy" part of the question became clear when she looked back at the email and saw the word wasn't really there.

I'm working too hard, she thought as she went back to the counter.

What's a retail girl gonna do, right?

It was Christmas Eve, and they were going to let three of the staff go at the end of the holidays.

She needed the job.

The answer to the "Newtonmas" part came later that night, when they were getting ready for the physics department's annual Christmas Eve party. The event would be held in their main offices. Given this was northern Indiana and it was December, it was going to be cold outside, but there would also be thirty or forty people in a smallish area inside.

It made for tough choices.

Add in that she'd been dating Ben for six months and living with him for one, and that this would be their first office party together and she was already nervous. *Like hanging with a bunch of PhDs and post-docs is going to make everything else so much better,* she thought. In retrospect, her choice of World History as a major could probably have been improved on.

Ella was glad her parents couldn't see her now. She didn't want them—or anyone else, really—to think of her as just a clerk. Of course, thinking that way was embarrassing too. The girls at the store were great. But, like everyone else she knew, Ella had always expected more of herself than working retail. There were no jobs for History majors here, though, and the whole question of who she was going to be when she grew up seemed to be smacking her in the metaphorical face every hour on the hour these days. Yes, overthinking everything was her superpower. She could do it falling out of bed.

She held a pair of blouses up to her torso.

"Which one," she asked, knowing Ben wasn't going to answer.

"I like them both," he said.

She picked the blue one because she thought it looked smarter.

"Newtonmas is a thing we're doing at school this year," Ben said, finally answering her question while he pulled on his only clean dress shirt. He used the *isn't this amazing* tone he always took on to explain stuff.

She was cranky enough she had to remind herself that his voice had been the first thing that caught her attention—that it had sounded warm and inviting rather than condescending, and that it made her think he could see big things in little places.

"It's going to be great fun," he said, explaining that Sir Isaac Newton, of falling apple fame, had been born on Christmas Day back in the 1600s, and that, with three full weeks before classes started back, the department had decided it would be fun to celebrate all ten days—that being the span between Newton's Christmas birthdate by the Julian calendar, and January fourth, which was his birthdate by the Gregorian.

"Does that mean I get ten presents?"

"Greedy much?"

"More like desperate," she replied. "If we're not going big on Christmas, it's time to soak this Newton thing."

He laughed. "There might be more coming."

"And, not to complain, but if you're doing ten days, shouldn't you have sent my first present tomorrow?"

"I like to jump the gun," Ben said.

Which was true. He'd asked her to move in with him so quickly, for example, because he said it felt right. She agreed with that enough to say yes. He seemed like a great enough guy— certainly better than Carlo before. Ben was older than her, too, nearly thirty. He felt more stable. And, she could admit, it was great to cut rent in half. If she hadn't said yes, she would have needed to downsize.

"Anyway," he said, sweeping his arms wide. "The entire physics department has decided to be true Newtonians this winter break."

Ella didn't like the sound of that, but she was too stressed to deal with it.

But, at the party, it became clear he meant that the department members were going to meet on each of those ten days—like professors first did a long time ago. Ostensibly, they would discuss scientific things, but the vibe at the party said the sessions were more likely to be about spreading "good cheer" and bitching about the dean.

"You're going to leave me alone for ten nights?" she said later as he drove them back through snow-lined streets to the apartment. Her brain was numb from meeting so many new people. Her stomach was churning from dinner that, for her, had been mostly wine, dip, and crackers. Most of her friends had graduated and moved on. The idea of Ben stepping out on her made her unhappy.

"You can come with me if you'd like," Ben said.

She put her head back on the rest.

On Christmas day, Ella's "true love" gave her an Albert Einstein action figure. It was less romantic than the tone generator, but Ben didn't think so. They'd been out sledding earlier. It had been fun. Now they were back in their apartment, drinking hot cocoa and playing a game of Scrabble.

"Albert can be our first Christmas ornament together," he said as he bent Einstein's arm into a crook and looped it around a branch. "We'll put him right here."

Ella rolled her eyes. "This is what happens when you fall for a physicist?" she said.

He spread his arms wide. "Hey, it's all relative."

She sighed and thought about her family out in Colorado.

They would be getting together today. Aunts, uncles, and the handful of cousins.

Her family celebrated a staggered Christmas, meaning each branch held their own celebration on Christmas Eve, then gathered together for dinner and football the next day—today. Mom and Dad hosted the big get-together, so the house was always layered with Christmas cheer—holly and mistletoe, cinnamon-scented candles that would burn down to nothing by the end of the night, and a tree, of course, a live one that smelled like pine and was crammed full of lights.

She and Ben were invited, but Ben's classes had gone almost all the way to the holiday. And this was Ella's first year at the store. She couldn't afford to leave.

As stupid as it sounded, Ella thought she wouldn't miss it at all.

She'd told herself she'd stayed in Indiana because she liked the little college town feel of the place, but, as time passed, she knew it was other reasons, too.

She wanted to show she could make it on her own.

Which, of course, she wasn't.

Every time she thought of walking into the family den, she also fought down the certainty of how she would have felt to talk about her job at the store. She sighed, despite herself. No, the decision to stay in Indiana had been the safe one.

She missed presents, though, and the turkey and gravy, and, of course, the laughing. She even missed football.

"I thought this was Newtonmas," she said absently, looking at her Albert Einstein figure. "Not Einsteinmas?"

"I couldn't get a Newton soon enough."

She smiled and played a word. Yes, this is what happens when you live with a physicist.

He left after a quick dinner.

"Are you sure you don't want to come along?" he asked.

She shooed him away. "I've been waiting breathlessly to get you out of the place ever since you told me about it."

"I thought you were mad at me."

"I got over it."

Which was true. Once she stopped being angry, Ella began to look forward to having the apartment to herself.

It was pretty much great.

She put on some music, got into a pair of old sweatpants, and curled up on the soft sofa with a glass of wine and a plate of cheese. She picked up a book and got through most of it in one setting.

A half bottle later, she called up her email and followed the link Ben had sent yesterday.

It was a strange "gift"—just a site that played tones of any frequency she entered—but it got interesting after she discovered she could hear nearly up to the 18,000Hz range: 17,853 to be precise, which was pretty good. Ella didn't know how good until she checked the chart he'd attached, which said that some humans could hear up past 20,000 but most weren't capable of more than her—especially at twenty-five years of age, which she would be for another two months.

So much for her mom yelling at her for using ear buds.

She liked that she was exceptional. Or close to it, anyway. It had been awhile since she felt like that about anything.

"I've got good ears," she said to herself.

She thought about that as she played with the tone generator longer.

It was past midnight before she shut off her phone and lay in the darkness of the living room.

It wasn't long before she gave in to her exhaustion.

On the third evening of Newtonmas, Ella stopped at the grocery on her way back to the apartment. She'd worked late. Ben would be gone to his Newtonians thing by the time she got home. She was looking for a quick dinner.

She was also angry.

It was the day after Christmas, or, as her boss called it, Hell Day. Her feet hurt. Her back ached, and her brain was frazzled from saying "perhaps your sister has a receipt?" to one person after the next.

Then there was Mr. Bradford himself.

Standing in front of the grocery's freezer section, her thoughts kept looping back over their meeting.

They'd been alone in his cluttered little office, going over her final closeouts.

"You've got good figures," he said with an overlarge grin. He leaned back in his squeaky chair and put his interlocked fingers over his head. "You know we'll be cutting people after the new year."

"Yes," Ella said.

"Desi's numbers are pretty hot, too."

"I'm sure they are," Ella replied, not catching anything at first.

The pause had been just a little too long, though. Or had it been? Maybe she was making too much of it. Maybe not.

"You might start thinking about just how much you want to stay on," her boss had said then, the tone of his voice and the expression on his face carrying a chill that ran up Ella's spine. What was he saying? Anything? Nothing?

She'd been here for almost six months, and he'd never been out of hand before, but the words "figures" and "numbers" locked her brain up by jumbling together with "hot" and "start thinking about how much you want to stay on."

"I will," Ella said, unable to think of anything else.

All she wanted now was a frozen pizza for dinner, and more wine.

Yes.

Lots and lots of wine.

"Ella?" a voice interrupted.

Ella jumped in her own skin, and turned to find another woman about her age, hair dark like hers, but curled. Dark eyes. Bright cheeks.

"Hi," she finally said.

"I'm sorry to scare you."

"It's all right." Ella's laugh felt too nervous.

The woman looked familiar, but Ella couldn't place her.

"Fiona," the other said. "From Ben's physics gang?"

"Ah, yes! I'm sorry. I didn't recognize you away from the setting."

Their conversation had been a pleasant time. Her best talk of the night.

"Not a worry," Fiona said.

"You're a post-doc, right?" Ella said.

"Yes, spectroscopic lasers for trace gas detection."

"Sounds hard."

She smiled. "Yes, well, we can do hard things, now, can't we?"

Some of us more than others, Ella almost said.

"I guess," she replied instead. "Are you getting ready for the Newtonians tonight?"

"I'm thinking I'll do pizza instead," she said, her slight pause giving her away.

Ella relaxed a little. "Too much of the boys' club?"

"You could say that."

"You want company?" Ella said.

Until she'd said it, Ella wasn't sure she wanted company herself, but, as the words came out of her mouth, she realized just how much she craved talking with someone without any strings attached.

Fiona nodded as if contemplating.

"My oven's got two racks," Ella added. "And we can always get more wine."

Fiona smiled.

"Sure. I'd love to."

When they got back to the apartment, Ella found today's Newtonmas present in the mail. It came in a padded envelope addressed to her, and when she finally opened it, she discovered a package that included a prism, a mirror, and a compact disc.

A bit earlier, she'd received his email.

Happy Third Day of Newtonmas!

Here are your directions for the prism. Hope you have fun!

The email had links to experiments she could do.

She opened the package after getting the oven started and before opening the first bottle.

"That's cute," Fiona said as she played with the triangular crystal. "Ben's a good guy."

"Yeah, I suppose so."

"Trouble in paradise?" Fiona said.

"No. Not really. It's just ... well ... It's just gone pretty fast."

Ella handed her a wineglass, noting that Fiona let her comment go.

Fiona took the glass and raised it to Ella's. "Well," she said. "Here's to the Girl Newton club."

"I like that," Ella replied. "But I'm not sure I qualify."

Fiona noted the prism. "This is probably the only meeting in town with any physics going on."

Ella laughed, and peered at it. "Can you show me how to use it?"

"Sure. All normal lights have colors buried inside them," Fiona said. It was something Ella had known, but definitely not anything she ever thought about.

Thirty minutes later, Ella had learned how to make all sorts of rainbows, and the pizza was ready.

The cheesy dough and bit-of-everything toppings were exactly what her mouth needed, and, somehow, seeing the prism spread color against a series of backgrounds made her feel better.

"Thanks," she said as Fiona left the apartment.

"Same time tomorrow?" Fiona asked.

"Sounds great," Ella said.

On the fourth day of Newtonmas, before she left for work, Ben gave her a fun little gyroscope.

She liked twirling it on the counter as she ate breakfast. Liked how it always stayed in the right orientation no matter what happened around it. As fun as it was, though, it was the prism she'd taken to the store instead—partly because it fit into her purse, but just as much because she'd dreamt about rainbows last night. Before calling Fiona, she'd used it to scatter the flashlight of her phone against the wall.

They decided they would go to Mason and Taylor's, a local restaurant where the food was good and the prices at least somewhat reasonable.

"It still counts as Christmas, right?" Ella asked as they arranged their meeting time.

"Sure. Or, if it doesn't, we'll just consider it an official meeting of the Girl Newtons."

"Here's to a self-gift."

Ella ordered a Cobb salad and broiled cod. Fiona had chicken salad and fries.

"Are you okay?" Fiona asked.

"Yeah, why?"

Fiona looked at her, but didn't respond.

It had been another rough day. Bradford had ratcheted the pressure up with more borderline conversation, this time suggesting that Melanie's numbers were on the rise. Melanie was a first-year at school.

"I think I'm going to quit my job," Ella said.

As soon as she said it out loud, her throat seemed to choke up. No. She wasn't going to cry. Not here. She gripped the napkin in her lap and steeled herself as she blinked her eyes and took a breath.

"I see," Fiona said. "Want to tell me about it?"

It came out. Slowly and surely.

It even sounded like she was in control of herself, which made her happy.

"I can't tell if he's serious or not," Ella said.

"He's a cagey bastard, that's for sure," Fiona added. "But he sounds like a grade-A dick."

The set of her face suggested to Ella that Fiona had her own stories to tell. She was in a field that was still 80% male, after all.

Ella wasn't ready to ask her about them, though.

But hearing Fiona confirm her interpretation brought her situation to a head.

"Anyway," Ella said. "I'm thinking of quitting."

"What are you going to do then?"

Ella grimaced.

If she quit, she'd be stuck to Ben. The realization was a stab in the gut. She liked Ben. He was, as Fiona had said, kind of a great guy. How many other guys send their girlfriends goofy physics presents, after all? So, yeah, she liked him a lot. And it was possible she even loved him. But how could she know for sure? It had been so fast, which wasn't like her at all. She was the kind of person who took two weeks to decide on a dress, after all. Usually she needed time.

Then there was the question of whether he really loved her.

He'd been engaged before and called it off.

Sitting in the restaurant amid the smells of condiments and roasted meats and sounds of distant clatter, and with Fiona across from her with her open but inquisitive expression waiting, Ella knew she never should have moved in with him. Maybe someday, yes, but not now.

It wasn't fair. Not to him, and not to her.

And then there was Desi and Melanie, and the other girls in the store. Who knows what conversations Bradford was having with them.

She shuddered.

Quitting would mean leaving the rest of the girls to their own devices. She wanted to stay because she wanted to pull her weight, and she wanted to stay because she needed the goddamned job.

Either way, talking to Fiona had helped her come to at least one conclusion.

"I don't know," she said. "But I've got to do something. The alternative isn't acceptable."

"Can you go to his boss?"

"Without proof?"

Fiona nodded. "Sucks. What about the other girls?"

"No one has anything concrete. But they all know the deal. Three of us are walking in January. Everyone's on pins and needles."

Ella put her fork down.

"What do you do, Fiona? I know your situation is different. But it's not *that* different, right? what do you do when this happens?"

"Truth?"

"Yeah, truth."

Fiona took a deep breath, then let it out in a long sigh.

"I eat it. Every day. I wish I could say I was better than that. But..." She shrugged. "I guess I'm not."

Ella nodded. "Thank you," she said.

"I'm sorry it's not much help."

"Sure it is."

"Have you talked to Ben about it?"

"No," Ella said. "I don't know if he'd understand."

"That's fair. I mean, he's as dense as the next guy, I suppose."

Despite the lump in her stomach, Ella couldn't help but smile. "Aren't you Newtonians supposed to take each other's side?"

"Sure," Fiona said, reaching for her wine glass. "But I'm a Girl Newton, too. Kinda puts me in a bind."

"You should have thought about that before you went double agent."

They talked about other things through the rest of the meal.

Outside, it began to snow, so Ella told stories about sledding with Ben. Somehow the conversation moved to skiing with her family in Colorado. Eventually, Ella realized she'd been talking nonstop.

"I'm sorry," she said. "I just got caught up."

"Not a worry. I like hearing about your family."

When they left the restaurant, they agreed to meet again tomorrow.

"I'll host," Fiona said as she stepped away.

On the fifth day of Newtonmas, Ben gave her a flashlight.

It was early in the morning, which didn't surprise her because he'd come home earlier last night. "All we're doing is drinking," he said when she asked why.

"I'm sure you're doing it well, though," Ella said.

"It is a cross I bear."

Of course, he'd slept like a log while she just tossed and turned.

That morning, however, the Newtonmas gift was wrapped in a shoddy fashion, scotch tape everywhere. It came with a "Merry Newtonmas!" card, that had an apple tree printed on the front.

She'd had her coffee, but only a half-piece of toast.

All morning she'd been freaking over what to do when she got to work. Ben's adamancy that she open the gift now didn't help.

"Let me guess," she said, shaking the wrapped flashlight. "It's a telescope."

"Very close," he said.

"Did you just take it out of that toolbox in the closet?"

"Maybe," he said. "You'll have to open it to see."

She unwrapped it, saw it was, indeed, a flashlight, and gave it all the oohs and aahs it deserved.

"Close your eyes," he said, taking the flashlight from her.

"You're going to make me late," she said.

"That's all right. You can blame me."

His off-hand acceptance of said blame, and the fact that he didn't understand what he was saying just made her even more angry.

She closed her eyes, though.

"Keep them closed," he said. "I'm going to shine this on your eyelids. I want you to move your eyes around and tell me when you see your retina."

"My retina?"

Even upset, she could imagine his lips pulling back in a slow smile.

"Yes. Or at least the patterns of your blood vessels in them."

He put the light on her face, and her view flared orange and yellow. "Rotate your eyes around."

"This is stupid."

"Rotate!"

She rolled her eyes. "I don't see anything but orange blobs."

"Again."

She rolled them again and again until, all of a sudden, a pattern of delicate paths appeared across her view.

"Holy shit, that's cool."

He took the light away, and she blinked until her vision readjusted.

"It *is* pretty cool, isn't it?"

He gave her a kiss goodbye, and went to put the flashlight back.

"What do you think you're doing with that?"

He stopped, and the questioning expression on his face made her smile.

"I believe that's mine," she said. "You did just gift wrap it for me, right?"

He handed it to her swordlike, handle first and over his forearm.

"Milady," he said.

She took it with her, laying it on the passenger seat on her way to work.

Every time she looked at it, she thought about her retina, its small veins stretching out like a veil, filled with almost nothing, yet making it so that she could see all the amazing things there were to see. Each time she looked at it, she remembered the expression on Ben's face and the calm, regal way he presented the flashlight to her.

For the first time in a while, she felt almost good walking into work.

As luck had it, Bradford was out sick, so all her worrying was just pushed off a day.

Later that night, though, while having dinner, she showed the flashlight to Fiona.

"That's cool," she said.

"I know!" Ella replied.

"What's cool?" the waitress said.

Before they left, they'd done it with every waitstaff in the place.

The manager took 50% off their bill.

"I'm going to the boys' club tonight," Fiona called to say on the sixth day of Newtonmas.

"Turncoat," Ella said.

"They're beginning to miss me. How was your day?"

"Fine," she said. "Bradford was out sick."

"Small mercies."

When she got home, Ella discovered Ben had left a small box on the counter, wrapped in light blue paper. He'd written "Merry Newtonmas!" on the paper.

Inside were three chocolates and a note, but she found that the real present was the wrapping, which changed colors when she touched it. The note read: *Put me in the freezer.*

"Cute," she said, realizing she actually felt good today.

She put the paper in the freezer.

A few minutes later she fished it out to see new words under the original ink.

"Did you know you're hot?"

She actually snorted at that.

"You've said that before," she said to herself, grabbing a frozen dinner. Maybe tonight she could finish that book.

The seventh day's present was a Newton's cradle, which seemed appropriate—a complex pendulum of five hanging balls that knocked against each other, one side sending the other side flying. She left it on the coffee table, figuring this one was as much for him as it was for her.

Bradford was in, but only for half a day.

On the eighth day of Newtonmas, as they were gathering breakfast again, Ben gave her a clear two-liter bottle of water and one of those laser beams cats love so much.

"Shake it up," he said.

She did.

"Harder."

She did.

Then he motioned the laser. When she picked it up he turned off the light. "Shine on, baby," he said.

The result was a crisscrossing display of light.

She couldn't help giggling as she moved the beam around. "That's amazing. Almost like a disco ball. Is it just water?"

"Not exactly," Ben said.

"What's the secret ingredient?"

"If I told you, I'd have to kill you."

"I can Google it, you know? I have the technology?"

"Yes, but do you have the fortitude?"

She smiled and looked back at the bottle.

It was, admittedly, cool.

Mr. Bradford was in all day. Several times she gathered up her nerve and went to his door with plans to confront him, but she never stepped in. It wasn't about the job, now, she realized.

She could live with being fired.

The idea of the conflict, though, put a ball of dough in the pit of her stomach that made her heart crash against her throat. It was the fallout that kept her from knocking on the door. She didn't think she could handle what could happen next.

So instead, she just left.

"Give me your index finger," Ben said on the ninth day of Newtonmas. He was holding a sheet of wrapping paper. It was Sunday and she was off work. He had one more day before the semester started.

She was sitting on the couch, drinking coffee and staring out the window as the weather tried to decide whether to snow or not.

"My index finger?" she said.

"I am now of the understanding you have exceptional ears, so I assume you heard me the first time."

She stuck out her tongue, but capitulated by putting her cup down and giving him her index finger.

He draped the wrapping paper over it, and then secured it around her finger with tape.

"What is this?

"Merry Newtonmas!"

"I'm thinking you're getting cheaper every day."

"Newtonmas is, admittedly, a little pricey."

"Seriously, what is this?"

"Open it."

She shook her head, but pulled the paper off. "Amazing. It's my finger. How did you know I always wanted one?"

"My dear, I present to you the greatest muscle measurer on the planet!"

"Underwhelming."

"All you have to do is put it in your ear."

She gave her best doleful stare.

"I'm serious."

"You're insane."

"I've heard that before, but for now you're going to put your finger in your ear and listen."

Several seconds of silence ensured.

Finally, she put her finger in her ear.

"Leave it there," he said. "Let it get steady, so you can ignore the sounds your movement makes."

"All right," Ella replied, feeling silly. The sound was raspy.

"What do you hear?"

"It's kind of like an echo. Or a hum."

"That's right. Now, keep your finger in your ear and clench the muscles of your arms. That hum will change."

"Amazing," she deadpanned.

"Did it change?"

"Yes."

"Do you know why?"

"Given your lede, I assume it's my muscles."

"Exactly. It's the muscle fibers in your arms twitching. Thousands of them. Millions. On and off again."

She actually smiled.

He looked at her, his expression suddenly more steady and firm than before. The change caught her up. Without knowing exactly why, she found herself focused on him.

"You're a strong woman, Ella," Ben said then. "Whatever's going on, you can handle it."

"What?"

"Look, I know I've been gone a lot for the last week and a half, and maybe it's not even my place, but I don't need to be a Nobel winner to know there's something bothering you. I just want you to know that you're exceptional in hundreds of ways. Not just your ears. Which are amazing, by the way. Whatever it is that's going on, I want you to know that you are amazing both inside and out."

Ella blushed.

"If you want to talk about it, I want to listen."

"Are you sure?"

"As sure as I can be."

She looked at him then, and the world stopped. Yes, she thought as she took in his dark eyes and felt the thin creases in the corners of those eyes, Ben Stiles was a good guy, a guy who gave her goofy presents, but he was more than that. Ben Stiles was a man she could trust.

"All right," she said.

Then she started talking.

When they were done, Ella knew two things.

The first was that she was going to do something more with her life. She would go back to school. Maybe start a business. She didn't know exactly what she was going to do, but she had time to figure it out.

Even if she kept her job for now, she wasn't going to be working at the store much longer.

The second thing she knew was that, if she had any say in it at all, neither would Butch Bradford.

At first, Ella considered wearing a wire. She thought about creating a scene where Bradford would incriminate himself, imagining how he would take his step too far, and how she would enjoy that delicious moment when she revealed he was going to be crushed.

But no.

Too many things could go wrong if she taped him.

And, in fact, the mere act of recording Bradford covertly could make her the villain.

She'd seen it before.

She had a vendetta, Bradford would argue. She was devious and conniving! Just listen to her on the recording! Hear how she led him on? She was just a pissed-off employee who wasn't doing her job. And she was desperate. She would do anything to keep her job.

Bradford had been with the company for twelve years without a complaint, he'd say.

He'd explained that her position was being vacated after the holidays, and now she was making a last-ditch effort to take him down with her.

No, if Ella recorded him, she would be the one blamed.

She considered going to the chain's Human Resources department. But then she considered the other women on the team: Desi and Melanie who needed their jobs just to live, and the others. And she remembered the look on Fiona's face the time she talked about her situation. Fiona, who worked in a field as bent against her as any other. They were all silent because they knew how things were slanted.

So, yes, Ella would use the system if she could, but she knew going to HR alone wouldn't solve the problem.

She had to face this head-on.

She had to stand up to Butch Bradford.

Which is how she found herself standing outside her boss's office early that afternoon.

The door was closed, but Ella could hear him rustling inside, his chair giving small groans as he moved around.

She thought of Ben then, and the string of Newtonmas presents he'd given her.

She had exceptional ears, she thought.

The veins in her retinas were amazing.

Standing there, she swore she heard the firing of muscle from along her arms.

The last image that came was the gyroscope as it had spun so perfectly on the breakfast table this morning. It was still one of her favorite things, mostly because she had no idea how it worked.

She dried dampness from her palms and pushed open the door.

"Ella?" Bradford said.

She shut the door behind her.

"What's up?" Bradford said, his eyes wandering to her chest as he sat back. She'd worn a pair of dress slacks and a company shirt, only one button undone. A small aquamarine necklace was her only jewelry.

The gaze annoyed her.

She pulled the chair from beside him to the opposite side of the desk, then sat down.

His eyes narrowed, then widened.

I can do this, she thought as she waited silently.

The sound of the ventilation system rose in the background, and the pressure of her silence raised questions in his gaze. She'd heard from her father that in this kind of stand-off, the first person to move was going to lose.

"What can I do for you, Sweetie," he finally said.

"You've got to be better than that, Mr. Bradford."

"Better?"

"I wanted to talk to you about the job," she said.

His smile grew relaxed, almost familial, and, as he became more comfortable, Bradford let his gaze focus once again on the gem at the hollow of her neck again, then move down.

"It's going to be a *stiff* race, Ella," he said. "I don't mind saying you've got a lot of very *hot* and *motivated* competition, if you know what I mean. I've got a real *hard* decision to make."

"I know all about my competition," Ella said. "That's what I wanted to talk to you about."

Bradford's gaze went to the closed door, and more calculations went off in his mind. Ella had closed the door firmly to make a point.

They were alone.

Anything could happen.

It was clear Bradford had gotten the gist.

He pushed the chair back to create space between himself and the desk. His arms fell to the rests. His smile became something deeper, and his legs gave a slow but perceptible spread.

"So, just what did you want to *say* to me about the job?"

Only partially able to ignore her anger, Ella reached into her back pocket and pulled out a creased sheet of paper, hoping the shaking of her hand didn't get any worse.

Gyroscope, she thought before proceeding.

"I wanted to say that by my count we have eleven people in the department. Fourteen if you count the overnight stockers."

"Yes?"

"I've spent the morning talking to every one of them, and, after they all agreed to forgo overtime, I've created a schedule by which all of us can keep our jobs."

Ella turned the paper around and slid it on top of Bradford's other work.

Bradford sat up, perplexity showing on his expression.

"All of us except you, that is," Ella added.

"What?"

"You're going to resign, effective today."

He laughed. "Is this some kind of a joke?"

"No, Butch, this is no joke. This afternoon, me and four of the other women you've been badgering are going to make reports to HR," Ella said without breaking her calm. "All of us who can afford to live without this shitty paycheck, anyway."

"HR?"

Bradford was leaning full forward now, perched on the edge of his seat. Color rose to his cheeks as he absorbed what she was saying. Bradford's voice grew stronger and it was like his entire body got bigger.

"Are you out of your mind, Ella? This is insane."

"I don't think so."

"Are you asking to be fired right now? Because you know I can do that, right? I can make that happen in a blink."

Gyroscope, gyroscope, gyroscope, she thought before speaking.

"If you resign, it will stop there. We just want a trail started so your next place of employment knows what they're getting into. But if you don't resign, not only will we all make these reports, but the four of us will also take our story public. It will be all over my social media, and on local news if they'll carry it. Every employee here will know what you've done. Your friends. Your family. Once it gets outside these walls, neither you nor I can control it. It's your choice, Butch. Resign and it will just go on your work record. Don't resign, and we will make a stink I don't think you will like."

"This is blackmail."

"And what you do is harassment."

"Come on, Ella," Bradford said.

She watched him reassess her, reconsider the fact that she was an educated woman even if she was more than a little unassuming. "This is all a big joke, right? I'm not that bad. I mean, I know I'm a little loose with the language sometimes, but—"

"Donna Mears."

"Donna Mears?"

"Do you need your ears checked?"

"Who the hell is Donna Mears?"

"Isabelle DiCenzo. Karla Jones. Sandra Jane Lehman."

The names began to register. They were all women who had worked here over the past several months. Part-timers. Nobodies in the big picture. Women who needed the money, women who told Ella they'd been in this office with the door closed themselves.

"To be honest," Ella said. "When I first thought this through, I figured you'd keep your job. Everyone deserves a second chance, right? But then the girls got to talking and we saw just how long it's gone on."

Bradford reached for the phone.

"I'm calling security right now."

"Go ahead," Ella said so calmly she nearly high-fived herself. "It's your life, Butch. We're just giving you a choice on how you want to live it."

Her boss sat back, still contemplating, but defeated.

Ella stood up and opened the door.

"Don't worry about the shop," she said. "We've got the new work schedule posted. We'll be fine until we can find a replacement."

Then she stepped out of her boss's office.

She had a report to make.

The orange sun was just setting when Ben took Ella to the sledding hills again.

The reports had been made.

Butch Bradford had been called on the carpet, and had resigned.

Ella had no idea who the new boss was going to be, nor, right now, did she really care. She'd done it. She'd found something inside her, something that had always been there but that she hadn't been able to connect with. The world was bigger than her, but she had a part to play, even if she wasn't totally sure what that part was going to be.

Now the chilled air was fresh against her cheeks and the sound of high school kids whooping and hollering pierced the evening as toboggans and rounded sheets of metal crunched down the snowy slope.

In a few minutes the sun would be gone.

Soon there would be stars.

She couldn't think of a more perfect way to end the day.

"Let me teach you how to get dizzy up and down," Ben said as they stood at the top of the hill. Their breathing left white clouds to swirl around before disappearing into the cold air.

"Dizzy up and down?"

"Yes. It's totally different from getting spun round and round, you know?"

"You are a bona fide dork," she said with a smile.

He just nodded and kept on.

"It has to do with the different equilibrium loops in your ears. You've got three of them. I can promise that the sensation is quite delightful." He smiled then, showing her how. "Put your head to the side first, like this, then spin like you would normally."

He spun around, and promptly fell to the snow.

He got up, brushing snow from his pants.

She tried it, and fell hard, laughing, into the padding of snow. "It *is* delightful," she finally said. "Totally different."

He dropped down beside her, then gave her a kiss.

He reached into his pocket and retrieved a small blue box, which he then opened to reveal a ring, glistening brilliantly white from its velvet backing.

"What's this?" Ella said.

"Technically," he said, "it's pressed carbon and gold."

She hit him with a handful of snow, laughing again.

"Haven't you already given me my ninth day?" She twirled her gloved index finger in the air and stuck it bluntly into her ear.

"Yes, but you know I like to jump the gun."

"So this is my tenth day of Newtonmas?"

"Sure," Ben said, holding the ring box up.

The diamond caught the last rays of the setting sun to create colors.

"Will you marry me?"

"Yes," she said as quickly as she could.

Then she kissed him, and he kissed her, and though she was sure that, somewhere, a gyroscope was spinning, all she could think of now was this amazing kiss, the dazzling display of stars that would accompany their walk home, and that perfect rainbow of color sprayed out across the snow.

The idea behind "The Year That Went into Extra Innings" originated at the workshop where most *Fiction River* stories are reviewed, discussed, and selected. Kris had finished her process of sorting, and was still needing space filled. During a break, Brigid asked if I'd collaborate on an idea she had (at least I'm pretty sure it was her idea rather than mine). Long story short, Brigid pitched it to Kris, Kris said to go for it, and voila! "The Year That Went into Extra Innings."

I think it's pretty much a quintessential collaboration between us. Equal parts baseball and charming (you can guess which of us contributes which, right?). As I read it again it brought back memories of the glorious day that my wife and I took a ten-ish-year-old Brigid to Wrigley Field to watch our beloved Cubbies play ball.

The Year That Went into Extra Innings

Brigid Collins and Ron Collins

The World Series finishing on my birthday was—theoretically—the best gift I could have asked for, even if it meant me and Jake would have to shut down trick-or-treating early. Jake, the little booger he was, complained all day, of course, but I was thirteen now, not a little girl anymore. I had my priorities as straight as the bill of my Cubbies cap.

The weather was perfect that night. Crisp and cool with a gentle wind to left, as Jim Deshaies, the only voice of the Cubs that mattered, would say. I could smell sugar pops and chocolate under the wood smoke on the breeze. Leaves skittered across the sidewalks with an exciting sound of fall. Good for baseball, bad for reeling in a hyperactive kid brother from his candy collecting gig, especially when the brat kicked my shin (*It was an accident!* he yelled, but I know it wasn't).

"It's game seven," I said as I grabbed the puffy shoulders of his Batman costume and dragged him up the street.

"It's still light out," he whined, pointing at the orangey pink smudge on the horizon. "And they're just gonna lose, anyway."

I gritted my teeth against a childish outburst. No point in denying I was dreading this game.

The Cubs were hosting the Angels. They'd already blown game six.

I'd known what was going to happen even before Lester wound up and delivered the fastball that Mike Trout put into the lap of a half-drunk Bleacher Bum. The Cubs were going to choke. After being up three games to one, my team—heck, my whole family's team—was going to lose game seven.

Still, we had to deal with the crud, as Dad said. We *had* to watch.

That's what being a grown-up, die-hard fan meant.

I get it from Mom. For example, last year I'd decided on going out as Kris Bryant, but Mom said no way in hell. Bryant was probably going to be a free agent soon, and she wasn't having a turncoat trick-or-treater in the family. It was Ernie Banks, Ryne Sandberg, or Sammy Sosa—take my pick.

We got home in time to cram down a spaghetti dinner (my birthday, my favorite) and birthday cake chaser during the pre-game show. I blew out all the candles, and though I didn't tell, I suppose everyone knew what I was wishing for.

Me and Mom settled on the couch together, while Dad sat on the floor and helped Jake sort through his smaller-than-normal haul. Dad teased about taking his Dad Tax.

"Hey," I said, holding my hand out. "I'm the adult who took the kid trick-or-treating this year. I should get the tax!"

"Sounds fair, Fred," Mom said.

Dad grimaced, but agreed. "You know the deal, Jake," he said.

Jake threw a lemon lollipop at me and it hit me on the forehead.

"Ouch!"

He stuck his hateful little tongue out. In the past we've been pretty good together. He's really not a bad kid—I mean, if you had to have a little brother, Jake was acceptable. But he was getting worse as he got older, and this past few months was the worst of the worst. Now he was an eight-year-old demon.

To prove how deep it goes, Jake knows I hate lemon.

As the game started, I tried to ignore him. Tried to focus on what was important. Tried to not notice the taste of birthday cake rising in my throat. What if the old curse came back? What if the Cubs went another 108 years before they won it all again? I did the math and realized I wouldn't even be alive when that happened. A quick glance at Mom where she sat perched on the edge of the couch, elbows on her knees, hands clasped against her mouth showed me she was making similar calculations.

Don't let the Cubs blow it. Not this year!

When we went up 1-0 after one, and 3-0 after three, I began to believe.

But Trout did his Grand Slam thing, and we were down 4-3.

It stayed there through six innings, and then seven. We got a runner on in the 8th, but he got picked-off a pitch later and I thought Mom might well need to be sent to a hospital. Dad was in more control. The vein pulsing in his temple was accompanied by silent stewing rather than a scream and the tossing of the couch pillow across the room.

Which brings us to the bottom of the ninth, down a run with two outs and no one on—two ball, two strike count to Rizzo. One more strike and the season was over.

My heart hammered in my throat, and I swear all four of us had stopped breathing.

The pitch came. Slider. Down and in.

Riz clubbed it like a golfer, and the ball rose up into the dark Chicago night. The crowd roared, but none of us heard it because Mom and me, Dad, and even Jake, we were all screaming and jumping up and down amongst Jake's forgotten candy hoard. Rizzo, the Mighty Rizzo, had definitely *not* struck out. Instead he ran the bases and scored the tying run. One pitch later, the inning was over, but the game wasn't.

Oh no. My first year as an adult may have just started, but Game Seven was nowhere *near* over.

They played until the eighteenth inning that night before the game was suspended. The Angels scored a run in the fourteenth, but the Cubs tied it back up. Same thing happened in the seventeenth.

"You're killing me, Smalls," I said as I lay in bed that night, trying to sleep.

School the next day was hell. Everyone talked about the game. Jake sat next to me on the bus, quietly, which I admit always makes me nervous these days. The teams were going to start up again at noon—and rumor was that it would be shown on TV during lunch, and even longer if you had P.E. (which boiled down to saying Coach George was going to watch the game, regardless).

I had just finished entering the combination of my locker during passing period when Kendra Sax, whose locker was beside mine, said, "There's Tommie Williams" over the din of the chaos in the hallway.

I opened my locker and turned toward him in a single motion that was more a reaction than a thought.

She was right.

Tommie Williams—complete in his Cubs hat and Javy Báez jersey—was coming from down the hallway. We had been having a love/hate relationship for most of the past two years, meaning I both loved him and hated him because basically he was smart—for a boy, anyway—and he was cuter than I wanted to admit. He was also a player on the basketball team and had girls all over him. I wanted to be mature about things, though, so I tried to just ignore that. Tommie was a friend, at best. We cracked jokes and made fun of each other. That was my formal position as far as me and Tommie Williams were concerned.

The past two weeks he'd been coming around a lot, though, and with the winter dance coming up, Kendra had been teasing me that Tommie was going to ask me out.

"Hi, Tommie," I said, pressing books against my chest. He looked great in his Cubs gear. He was a big fan, of course. Which would obviously be a winner with my parents.

"Hi, Gail," Tommie replied.

His eyes went to a place behind me, then, and his face kind of froze, his eyebrows clenching together. He gave a double-clutch, like he'd been intending to stop and talk, but then moved on down the hall.

"What the hell was that about?" I said to Kendra.

Her gaze had gone to my locker, and her face blanched.

I turned and saw why.

The inside of the door was pasted full of pictures of the Angels' Mike Trout, and big dopey pages full of hearts colored in red and pink marker. "Mrs. Gail Trout" had been written about a hundred times in an awkward hand on note paper taped in a haphazard mess around the inside of the cubby.

I turned once again to see Tommie disappearing into the throng of kids.

Heat rushed to my face.

"Jake!" I said with too much force.

I was going to kill him.

The only thing that saved his life that day was that the game kept going on. From noon until midnight. Twenty-three more innings.

When they suspended play this time, the score was knotted at 11 apiece.

Lucky 11, I thought.

Tomorrow we'd win.

It was Thursday, late afternoon, and, in preparation of Thanksgiving feast, me, Mom, and Grandma were setting TV trays around my grandparents' cramped living room.

Usually, Thanksgiving was my least favorite school break.

Sure, you get three days off from school, but instead of hanging out with friends you have to drive five hours crammed into the back seat of Dad's Fiesta with the extra luggage and with

Jake's sprawl before being subjected to a long weekend with grandparents who insist on behaving like you're still interested in My Little Pony or Rainbow Brite, like I ever *was* into that stuff. Judicious amounts of pumpkin pie was all that got me through it most years.

Worse than that, Jake had a cold and was coughing all over me every step of the way—on purpose, of course.

But at least this year, there would be baseball.

Because a month after game seven had started, it was still going on. Except for two rain days and one the teams had agreed to take as a day off, the World Series played every day. It was amazing. Suddenly, instead of "Nice weather we're having, eh," people greeted each other with "How about that Series!" All the major league baseball honchos got together with the player unions and even made up special rules for how the Angels and Cubs could change their rosters and use their pitchers, and suddenly everyone was buzzing about how long it might go on.

The Series even kicked football off television in prime time, which, temporary or not, automatically raised Thanksgiving in my personal pantheon of favorite holidays.

Today would start at the 415th inning. The score stood 38-38.

Dad and Grandpa had chased Grandma out of the kitchen and were working culinary magic that sent enticing smells of baking turkey, whipped potatoes with butter, and green bean casserole wafting out to the living room, where me, Mom, and Grandma were setting up the tray tables in a semicircle around the TV. Jake lay on the floor again, fiddling with his favorite dinosaur model. Stegosaurus. He said he liked the ridges on its back. Whatever. Being only eight, of course, Jake got bored once the game stretched into its second week. Rather than focus on it, he spent most of his time inventing new ways to get on my nerves.

I kept telling Mom, but all she'd do is ask how I was going to handle it.

"You're an adult now," she'd say. "You figure it out."

For some reason, "pound sense into him" didn't seem to be the right answer, though the day Jake put food dye in my laundry resulted in her giving the brat a talking to.

Anyway, I'd tried all the usual steps. Compliments. Bribery. Even staying out of his way. But still it seemed like every other day something happened that I knew was Jake being Jake. One day all my pens were gone. Then next my computer passwords didn't work. A couple days ago he told Sandi Meyers that I like her boyfriend. Before that he told Ms. Pandita that I probably cheated on my history test.

Looking at the dinosaurs made me suddenly nostalgic for the days when we might have been sitting on the floor together and playing with them. The fact that he was being so quiet made me suspicious as I settled into the chair and gazed at the pre-game show. If I tried to play with them today, I'd probably get a T. Rex between the eyes.

"What are you doing for Advent?" Grandma asked my mom from out of nowhere.

That was another thing that made Thanksgiving hard. While our part of the family had drifted from church, Grandma was still very religious. She'd already showed us her Advent calendar for the year and explained how she had the candles in the Advent wreath already set up in the front window. "It's going to be a lovely sight from the sidewalk," she said, excitedly discussing the times she felt were best for lighting it.

"I don't know," Mom answered as she settled a tray. She glanced to the television, then to Jake, who was still busy with his dinosaur. "Depends, I suppose. We'll probably go to church."

"Probably?"

"We've got a lot going on," Mom said, shrugging more with her voice than her shoulders. Even I could feel the deflection.

"I see," Grandma said. "Too busy to prepare for the Second Coming, but not too busy for the World Series."

"We'll pray every day," she said.

"I already do," I added unannounced.

Both women turned quizzical expressions toward me.

"I pray that the Cubs won't lose," I said, adjusting my cap and making my eyes wide as if that was the most natural thing in the world.

Both laughed, and I felt better.

Then Dad and Grandpa came in with steaming plates of turkey and stuffing, and the mood was back to normal.

Mom brushed a hair off her forehead and smiled at Dad as he put the plate on her tray. Grandma sat in her composed way, her thin hands salting her food. I'm not an idiot. I know what Advent means, and I know Grandma believes in ways I don't think Mom does.

Images on the screen made me think about how the Cubs had brought me and Mom together more than anything else—sitting and chatting about plays and players as the game went on. Mom had played fastpitch softball in college. She liked the game, and she liked that I liked the game. There was a feeling of hope to it that made me happy when I was just a kid, a feeling like, no matter what, you always got your chance. But now I looked at the weary expression Mom was hiding, and it felt like there was something more to it for her.

It made me feel closer to her, that expression. Because baseball was becoming more for me than just a thing to get excited about all summer. Baseball, I was coming to realize, was a holiday of itself. It meant something, you know?

If you gave yourself to it, baseball was *worth* something.

There was a snow-out the first week of December, which apparently meant we had time to go to church once—which at least made Grandma happy, and which gave me an official place from which to make my request of God.

"Don't let the Cubs choke," I whispered to myself from the front pew.

It felt strange being here now. When I was a little girl I always felt the holiness of the church looming over me, but now I wasn't sure. Now sitting here and praying for the Cubs felt kind of like I was living a lie.

I hadn't wanted to go, but Mom had been firm: No get-out-skis.

Even Jake's wailing hadn't deterred her, and wonders be it seemed like at least sitting in church while the minister droned on served to keep him silent for a while. I'd forgotten he could sit still.

So, yeah, it felt strange to be here and be asking for help with something as inconsequential as the Cubs. Like they weren't something that should matter. But they did. They mattered to me, anyway, as I'd realized at Thanksgiving, and, from the way people kept talking it, they mattered to other people too.

God should understand, right?

I mean, do I really have to ask God to help starving kids, or families in need? God should just know about them, right? If God was real, which sitting here now I suddenly realized I wasn't actually sure about, well, if God was real She should take care of the poor and the sick whether I ask or not—otherwise, what good was She? But the Cubs are something God might overlook. That was how I looked at it, anyway.

Help the poor, I added, though, just to cover the bases, *but don't forget my Cubbies!* Then I threw in *Please!* Just to be sure.

No. I'm not proud of myself.

Would it work? I had no idea. But when the service was over, I saw I wasn't alone in my prayers. Tommie Williams was there with his family, Cubs cap in his hand, looking about as sheepish as I felt.

Whenever the snow cleared and the game started again, it would be the 523rd inning. The score was knotted at sixty-two runs each.

It was Friday, December twentieth, 3:17 in the afternoon, or—in other words—two minutes past the Freedom Bell that had just rung to release us for the full two weeks of Christmas vacation. The entire school was vibrating with energy so bold you could smell the lightning essence of adrenaline pulsing on the air. Kids screamed at the top of their lungs while they sprinted up the hallway, carrying projects in their arms, wrapping themselves in scarfs, and crashing into each other as they ran to the buses.

Tonight would start the 912th inning. Darvish was back on the hill. I felt good about our chances.

I crammed books into my locker and pushed my Cubs cap hard down onto my head to make sure it wouldn't jostle free in the scrum. Tommie was coming back around, and I'd made sure he'd seen it every day in December, but the fact was that I'd started getting more interested in Ben, a guy from my Spanish class.

"Did you hear Annie and Sam are doing a ritual tomorrow?" Kendra said from the locker beside me.

"Seriously?" I said.

"Our resident pagan strikes again!"

"Well," I flashed on how I'd felt when Mom and Grandma had their quiet, little spat, and also how it had felt in church a couple weeks back, "it *is* winter solstice now, and that's their jam."

"Yeah," Kendra said, showing she knew she'd been caught out. "And Annie is cool."

"It might be fun to go."

"Maybe for you."

I nodded, seeing a cross between exasperation and ironic patience crawl over her expression. Kendra's family was Jewish, and fairly strict about it. She'd invited me over for the afternoon at her place on Monday, which was the day after Hanukkah started, and I'd invited her over to watch the game the following day, assuming it was still running—or just to hang out otherwise.

"Solstice on Saturday," I said. "Hanukkah Sunday, and a run-up to Christmas on Monday and Tuesday. Your mom would be cool with it."

"Maybe."

"If you want to go, I bet I could get my mom to take us."

She smiled. Our moms had each other's backs. I didn't need to tell Kendra that if Mom was in on it, her mom would be chill. "I think that could be cool."

"I'll text you when I can ask her."

With that, I stood on my tiptoes and scanned the hallway.

"Have you seen the brat?" I said.

Kendra scanned, too. "Nope."

I always waited at my locker for Jake to arrive so I could make sure he got to the bus safely. That was my job the past two years since he started going to my school. He always came directly here.

"Maybe he's got caught up in traffic," Kendra joked, noting the wave of kids that still poured through the hallway.

"He better be quick, or we'll miss the bus."

"I'll see you later," Kendra said, leaving for her own bus. "Text me!"

"I will."

I stood there. Waiting. Five minutes later, the crowds had thinned, but still no Jake. Frowning, I walked toward his room. First and second grade are on the first floor, the middle school sections on the second and third. I took the central stairs, which are big, double-wide passages with marble steps. The clock read 3:25. The bus would be leaving in less than five minutes. Where the hell was he? Just like him to be late on the last day of school. Probably hiding on purpose to make me angry.

"Jake?" I called, but the hallway was empty enough that my voice echoed and drew stares from the three kids who were still there.

Suddenly I started to get worried.

What if he wasn't hiding?

What if?

I stepped quicker down the hallway to Mr. Francis's room, where Jake would have come from. Mr. Francis was there, seated behind his desk and reading something on a computer screen, his dark blue sweater neatly arranged over his slightly bulging belly.

"Gail?" he said when I stepped into the room. "How can I help you?"

"Is Jake here?" I said.

He pulled the reading glasses off his nose. "Jake? No."

"I can't find him anywhere," I said, suddenly completely afraid.

Mr. Francis called the front desk. Several other teachers seemed to teleport in. Principal Davis arrived a moment later.

"Stay here, Gail," Mr. Francis said, leaving me in the room. "We know what we're doing."

As they scoured the entire floor, and then the entire building, my heart started beating faster than it ever beat before. I sat alone in the room, thinking about my little brother and his love for his dinosaurs and …

Where could he be?

Did someone …

No.

I couldn't think about that.

Should I call Mom now? What would I tell her? *I'm sorry, Mom, but I lost Jake?* I felt heat rising to my face and it got really, really hard to breathe.

Ten minutes later, they received a return page from our bus driver.

Jake was there.

My first thought was relief, but that was quickly replaced by anger.

The snot-nosed brat. The little twerp.

I could see his face now, laughing at me.

He'd left me alone on purpose. Even though later he told Mom that he'd told me to meet him at the bus, I knew with a certainty purer than a John Lester slider that he'd gone straight to the bus without telling me. He'd left me to worry about him, and to look like an irresponsible fool.

This time I was most definitely going to kill him.

Luckily for him, Mom got to him first. By the time Dad picked me up after work, Jake was up in his room, grounded, his door closed, and the big KEEP OUT sign he'd put up there at the beginning of the school year acting as a shield.

The game was going to restart in a minute, but I went in anyway, shutting the door behind me so we were alone.

"Go away," Jake said. He was sitting on his single bed and had a Pokémon game in his hand.

I sat at the foot of the bed, not saying anything, but feeling the heat of anger flowing from him. So much for being grown up. Here I was, all supposedly adult and I didn't have a clue about what to say.

"You're going to miss the game," he said abruptly.

"Why do you hate me?" I blurted.

He looked at me like I had horns growing out of my cheekbones. "Because you hate me."

"No, I don't."

He chuffed and focused on his game. The tinny chimes coming from the speakers were too cheerful, despite the angry way he ground his thumbs against the buttons.

"Seriously, Jake. Why do you think I hate you?"

"You always talk to your friends about how great it is to be getting older, and you call me names when you talk to them and you make a big old deal about having to take me to the bus and to go trick-or-treating or anywhere else. I'm not stupid. You hate me."

Jake's eyes got hard then, and water glistened in them.

I started to argue with him, started to tell him that we were buddies and that I loved him because—well, duh—he was my little brother, but then I saw he was right.

That's exactly what I was doing.

"I'm treating you like a little kid," I said. "Making you feel like you don't matter to me."

Jake seemed to relax, which made me realize he'd been braced, like he'd been waiting for me to yell at him or to tell him how wrong he was.

"I'm leaving you alone too much."

"Yeah," he said, lowering the game.

"I'm sorry."

That's when he finally cried. One tear, dribbling over his red cheek before he wiped it clean with the sleeve of his Cubs shirt.

I scooted over beside him and opened my arms, hugging my little brother tight and feeling him breathe, letting him cry without me seeing him if he needed to.

"I'm sorry I went to the bus without you," he said.

I sighed.

"It's okay," I said. "You proved you can do it, though. You proved that."

"I wouldn't have gone if I didn't know how."

"I know."

It made sense now, though. The whole thing of Jake doing all these things to me. I'd left him behind, and that couldn't happen again.

"Look," I said, pulling away. "We're going to make a deal, all right? Me and you against the world. You're my brother, and I'm your sister. That's never going to change. If you make me mad, I'm just going to tell you about it, and if I make you mad, you're going to tell me, all right? No hiding things."

He nodded. "All right."

He wiped his nose against his sleeve again.

"You'd better go downstairs," he said. "Or you're going to miss the game."

I gave a devious grin. "Maybe we can just get it on the internet. Watch it together?"

"That could be done," he said overly calmly, pretending he hadn't been crying a moment ago.

We sat back on his headboard together like we had so many other times, and got the game on screen just as Kyle Schwarber was stepping to the plate. The score was 107 apiece.

"I'll go down and get popcorn and hot chocolate at the next break," I said.

"Awesome," Jake replied.

Kendra and I had a great time at Annie and Sam's solstice ritual. Hanukkah dinner at Kendra's was yummy, and early enough that I got home in time to see the game get to the 958th inning, in which the Angels' Shohei Ohtani hit into a double play to end a rally, and then Kris Bryant hit a ball that would have scored the winning run, only to have it get caught in the dead ivy along the wall.

Christmas came, and went.

Presents were opened, and dinner happened in front of the television again.

Still the game went on.

Inning after inning. When the Angels scored, the Cubbies scored. When they didn't they didn't. That's the thing about baseball, though. Like my Mom says, baseball's like life, it's not over until it's over.

Now it was December 31st.

New Year's Eve.

The ball had already dropped in Australia and China and Europe.

In Chicago, though, it was cold and clear, the game was getting ready to start, and the stands were filled to capacity once again.

"They just keep saying the same things," Jake said as the announcers spoke.

I shushed him without looking away from the screen.

His playful shove to my arm when I shushed him felt good. Things were getting better between us.

Mom came to stand beside me for a moment, then touched my shoulder. "Go help your father bring out the dishes, please."

My tray table had on it the pink plastic knock-off My Little Pony that Grandma had given me when we first stepped into her house for Thanksgiving. I remembered how accepting it with a graceful mumble of thanks had made me feel grown up, and realized I'd been right to feel that. Grandma had been proud of finding it, a little pony wearing a Cubbies hat, and with the team's logo stamped on its flank. To be honest, it *was* kind of cute, even though it had been made for six-year-old me rather than the thirteen-year-old version.

"I want to hear what they think of the roster changes," I said to Mom.

"I'll tell you if they say anything interesting."

I chewed my lip, but knew I had to go.

In the controlled chaos of the kitchen, I helped Dad make up four plates, putting heaping helpings of each dish on both Jake's and my own, then giving Jake extra green bean casserole, because, go figure, the kid likes green beans.

With a heavy, steaming plate in each hand, Dad and I filed back to the living room. The National Anthem was being sung as we sat and pulled our trays close.

"They're changing Rizzo out for Montgomery," Mom said. "He wrenched his shoulder yesterday."

Dismay made the whipped potatoes I'd just swallowed turn to paste in my stomach. Mighty Rizzo benched? "*Montgomery?* The guy hasn't played more than a handful of innings all season."

On that sour note, though, the game resumed.

It was 11:58 PM as the game turned to the bottom of the 1,044th inning. The score was tied, of course. Always tied.

Jake was slumped, asleep in the corner of the couch.

Dad was distracted, reading stuff on the internet as the game was playing. He was into a new show on Netflix, and following fan leads. The broadcast came back from commercial, and the announcers paused to officially welcome the New Year, then, after the cheering and the kissing and the singing of "Go Cubs Go," noted that, once again, the teams would play until 1:00 AM, or until the game ended, whichever came first.

"But whatever happens," Jim Deshaies said, "you can now officially say that this is the year that went into extra innings!"

I looked at Mom and smiled.

I'm not sure why, but as Javy Báez stepped to the plate, she held her hand out from across the couch, and I took it.

She squeezed me, then, and I felt how happy she was to be here. With me. With Dad and with Jake.

It's going to happen, I thought, feeling the warmth in her hand.

The game that started on my birthday was going to end.

Now.

The pitch came in.

The pressure of Mom's grip increased into a steady presence that I knew would be there forever.

Báez swung, and the bat gave a deep wooden crack.

And the ball lifted high and deep to left field

I wrote the first 400 or 500 words of this story a few years ago, and even shared them with a small writer's group I was working with. They all loved it and wanted to know what happened next for poor little Bobo. I did too. The story wasn't talking, though, so I set it aside.

Then Kris Rusch gave me the *Fiction River: Bloody Christmas* prompt, and the whole thing fell into my lap. I love it when that happens.

Bobo

It was the morning before Christmas when Bobo Kennedy found a phone under the trash bin out back of Nexus, a high-end restaurant on the north side of Chicago. She pocketed the device immediately, glancing down the alley for witnesses.

"Santa come early," she said, laughing to herself in a voice raw as concrete.

The coldness of the phone stabbed her thigh through the pocket, and her breath rasped in the hollow bin as she went back to search for bits of chicken or a half-eaten steak the rats might have missed.

Maybe she'd even find cranberry.

It was a cold December, even by Chicago standards. It hadn't snowed, yet, but a thin dusting of crystals cut swirling paths in the alley's currents. The grinding of tires on hard asphalt hissed from taxis as they passed down the way. A steady stream of people walked on the sidewalk, too, each hunched up in their coats and scarves, hats pushed on their heads and wreaths of misty breaths trailing behind as they strode by.

The food might be frozen, she thought, but it would still be good.

As she dug through the mess, however, she couldn't stop thinking about the phone.

Her body warmed it until it was just a steady pressure against her thigh. She wanted to touch it, wanted to look at it, but she didn't have much time because she was on Sister Fred's lot. Hiding it from him made Bobo feel like a bad because Fred was an old man. He'd had been in the streets longer than her, and had even taught Bobo some of his ways. Snooze you lose, though.

When she crashed against a sharp edge of the metal bin, however, she couldn't resist anymore.

Worried, Bobo removed one mangled glove, and pulled the phone from her pocket. She wiped grime from the surface and turned it over. It was smooth in her hand, silver on the back and rounded at the edges. It looked good. Not cracked or scratched.

Relieved, she peered at it closer.

She'd never had a phone like this, but had seen people staring at them, punching at them, preening to take pictures, or even sometimes speaking into them as they walked down the street. It had three buttons down one side, and another on the opposite. She pushed the one and cackled with something between fear and delight when the screen lit up with vivid blue light.

Rows of colorful symbols lined the display. Bobo recognized some words: Phone, Camera, and Photos.

Pictures! Even as a girl, she had always loved pictures.

She poked at the Photos icon like she'd seen people do, and a screenful of pictures showed up.

Bobo frowned.

The pictures were of papers, not people. Like pages of receipts, mostly.

She pushed at the screen several times, first expanding the document, next making it smaller. A few minutes later, she learned to scroll and saw there were other pictures. More documents. A letter. And more receipts.

Finally, she saw some real pictures.

The first was of a young woman. Probably not much younger than Bobo herself in reality, though they wouldn't look like it if you put them side-by-side. The woman was thirty, maybe thirty-five, with dark hair, brownish skin, and a toothy but shy smile. She'd taken the picture at home and was holding a present wrapped in green paper and a golden bow.

She just wrapped that up, Bobo thought. *She's happy.*

The next was a shot of a Christmas tree in a dark room with just its lights on. Red, blue, and green points flared on the screen. A few presents were underneath the tree.

The next was the same woman, this time with two girls, one a little older than the other. Maybe five and seven. They were in the kitchen and the girls were fighting over who would stir a pan of what looked like cookie batter.

Bobo crammed the phone back into her pocket, suddenly choking as the cold winter air bit into her chest. There were more pictures, but holding it suddenly made her feel bad. This wasn't her phone.

The facts of her situation came flooding back—the cold air, the wind, and the cracked concrete alongside the dumpster bin.

"Hey, Bobo!"

She whirled to see Sister Fred ambling toward her, or, more correctly, toward the garbage bin she was standing by.

She picked up the ratty duffle bag that held her things, then started walking the other way.

"What the hell you doin'?" Sister Fred said.

"Nothing, Fred," she called back. "I ain't doing nothing."

Further west, a dark limo rolled to a stop.

When the door swung open, Johnny "Two Bones" Bracca stepped into the void inside. The car drove away.

Johnny straightened his jacket and settled into the seat facing backward as the car rolled, then looked across to see Arturo Cametti watching him. The compartment was warm enough to make his cheeks glow after being in the cold. Outside, a Christmas tree in a store window slid silently by.

"Merry fucking Christmas, eh, Boss?" he said.

Johnny was thirty-two. He had known Arty Cametti since they

were playing stickball in the streets. A lot can change in twenty-five years, though.

"How did it go?" Cametti said.

"Good," Johnny replied. "It went good."

"Where is she?"

"Down in the basement, ready to talk."

"Complications?"

"It was clean, Arty. No one in the alley. No sound. Nothing to worry about."

Johnny relived the thrill of stepping out in front of the car in the middle of the alley, and seeing the woman step out of the driver's side. She was alone, like he expected. Shorter than he thought she'd be, though. Professional women were supposed to be tall and thin, and this woman was short, hunched over in her winter coat. Her and her skin were both dark in the shadows of the alley, but he saw the flash in her eye that said she was the right one. The woman thought he was there to tell her something about Arty and Big Cal Johnson, a guy the cops had down in the jail waiting arraignment. Instead, he hit her upside the head like she was a big boy, then when she was down on the ground wrapped the ether rag around her until she went out. Only took a minute.

"You're a good boy, Johnny Bracca."

"Thanks."

Still, the tone of his old friend's words made Johnny's stomach uneasy. The air was stagnant as they drove. The only sound was the heater pushing air.

The plasma screen beside him glowed with images that made the darkness feel like some kind of mystical light show. That was the thing about this time of year, with its snow flying and ice crystals growing in the corner of every goddamned window. Everything could be pretty if you let it be, as Victoria always said. He didn't fucking deserve her, but who was he to mess with the Big Guy in the Sky's plans, right? She knew he'd be coming home hungry after a long night, and she'd be waiting for him with the coffee and the eggs. The kids would already be gone to Granny's for Christmas Eve, so maybe she'd be up for a roll, too. Ho, ho, fucking ho.

Still, the expression on the boss's face wasn't right. Arty's eyes had grown hard like a shark's. His lips pressed into a line. As seconds ticked off, Johnny came to feel like a boulder was sitting squarely on his forehead.

"Something wrong, Arty?"

"Solomon went through her stuff, Johnny."

"And?"

"Solomon and me, we were looking for a phone, and there ain't no phone in the bag you delivered."

Johnny held his palms up. He knew better than to skim off a mark.

"I put everything in there and delivered it just like you told me."

Arty stared him down.

"I swear it, Arty. I got nothing."

"I believe you, Johnny. But you know what's on that phone."

"I don't know what to say, Boss."

He knew what was *probably* on the phone. Pages of financial documents. Money in, money out. Bank accounts that got twisted around other bank accounts hard enough that it made Johnny's head go into knots if he thought about it too much. Someone said the woman got pictures of a couple stiffs, too. Regardless, the woman had been poking where she shouldn't ought to poke. That much Johnny knew for sure. Given his job, that's all he really needed.

"What about her car, Johnny."

Johnny swallowed, feeling his saliva thicken. He'd shoved the woman into the trunk and driven her car to the basement. The body guys would take care of it from there.

"I looked it over. Standard rich chick, right? Silver Lexus. Lawyer or something, right?"

"Yeah," Arty replied. "Or something."

"Nothing left in it when we was done."

The limo rolled on in silence, light from the TV flickered over Arty's face. The skin of his face draped over his cheeks like crepe.

"Could she have thrown anything out, Johnny?"

Johnny shrugged and cleared his throat.

"Think about it," Arty said. "Think about it very hard."

"Yeah," he said, not knowing if this was the right answer or not. "Maybe she could have."

Arty nodded. "The cops will know she's missing soon, if they don't already."

"I'll find it," Johnny said, knowing for sure *that* was the right answer. "I got a guy in the phone place," he said. "I'll lean him."

"That's a good idea, Johnny," Arty replied, still staring him down.

"And maybe I'll go check the alleyway again," Johnny added.

"Yeah," Arty said. "I like that idea, too."

The car stopped, and the door swung open.

She would take it to the phone store.

They would know how to find the woman.

It was a bit of a walk—all the way down Lake to State, then a block south, all done with her bag strapped to her back, but the weather was good enough, and at least moving would warm her up.

Her mind decided, she added energy to her stride.

She was short, but at one time powerful.

The gnawing at her stomach was better, and Bobo felt good about what she was doing.

She imagined the woman getting her phone back with the pictures of her girls, how the woman's grin would slide up her lips to bring out a dimple on her cheek. The idea made Bobo feel like she was Santa Claus carrying home a prize. Bobo didn't know how to use the phone anyway, and the memory of those two girls fighting over cookies reminded her of her own sister, who she hadn't seen since...well...when was the last time she'd seem Sarabeth?

After the second foster set.

That would be it.

Sarabeth and Barbara.

They were supposed to be together, but that didn't last.

She passed a street Santa, ringing his bell.

It was a sign.

Yes. She was a good girl.

She would give this phone back to the woman, and walk away like she didn't need anything, because that's what she was. A good girl. A good girl like Sarabeth was, a good girl like her Momma had told them all those times before.

City banners were flying from holders high on the street lights, flapping in a stiff breeze that cut into Bobo's cheeks, but she didn't care.

People approaching her parted as she walked, none looking at her.

That was okay, too.

It was how it was.

At thirty-three, she'd lived off the street for longer than she wanted to remember, longer than most everyone else she met here, including Boomer and Sister Fred. She knew the score.

People on the sidewalks had to keep their distance.

Partly for fear that she might be full of the crazies, and partly because seeing people with nothing made them uncomfortable—the idea that they might feel guilty if they didn't give her something was a true thing, and something Bobo played on when she was working. Guilt is powerful in a person with money, especially at times like Christmas. Some were angry, of course. There was blame in those eyes, as if she wanted to sit on the goddamned street on purpose. But fuck them. They don't know like she knows. Ain't no one goes to the streets because they want to.

But, one or the other, all these people shared one thing.

She saw it even though none of them could name it.

People were afraid of her because underneath that bravado or disdain, they knew they were only one accident, or one bout with something like cancer, or—like her and Sarabeth—one dead Momma away from being just like her.

That's how it was.

And, just like the grime that lined the creases of her hands, it had been that way long enough to know nothing was going to be changing anytime soon.

They couldn't accept that, of course, because to open their eyes to that truth, to accept they were all walking on a tightrope where one unlucky misstep could change it all, was too scary.

When she was younger, she'd thought badly of these people, but now she found their ability to look past her like she didn't exist didn't matter. She was who she was. And today, the fact that they couldn't see her being a good girl made her mission even more special.

I'm a secret Santa, she thought as she passed a Panda Express and a Dunkin Donuts that smelled so good that she about passed out.

When she was working, she liked to just sit in a place. Mostly because sitting in one place usually paid more, but also because she could usually find a place where she didn't have to smell food she couldn't have.

"I'm a good girl," she said out loud.

Finally, as the L-train rattled on the tracks above the street, its cars cram-packed with shoppers, Bobo turned the corner that led to the phone store. The train squealed as its brakes engaged. People stepped off.

It was Christmas Eve. The stores would be open late, and the money would be good.

She could eat then.

The phone store was just past a television network's office building. Its broadcasting center was on the ground floor, and you could look through the perfect glass walls—now decorated with icy fringes and a press-on collage of a sleigh and its reindeer—to see for free the broadcast being made. ABC-7, EYEWITNESS NEWS the big blue and white sign read over the windows. Inside, across the carpeted room, a pretty, blonde woman in pearls and a red dress sat next to a suited man and his green Santa tie. To their side was a big green screen. They were lit in a cone of light so bright it made Bobo think about the snow globe her Momma had got her for her last Christmas.

She wondered where the globe had gone.

As the woman in red spoke, an image flashed on the broadcast screen.

It was the woman.

From the phone.

Bobo froze.

It was a professional-looking headshot, but there was no doubt it was the same woman. Angela Petty, the words said underneath. A scrolling line under that went by too fast for Bobo to fully read, but she saw the word MISSING, and POLICE.

On the cold street outside, her heart clenched up.

Bad.

Bad, bad, bad.

She'd dealt with the police before. Dealt with authorities of all kinds. They were all bad, all saying they were on your side and just wanting what was best, but then they dumped you in places you didn't want to be. Bobo ran her fingertips along the outline of the phone in her pocket.

The word MISSING scrolled again.

Then LAWYER. And FBI.

None of them made her feel any better.

Bobo blinked her eyes against the cold.

If she gave them the phone, they would do bad things to her. Maybe lock her up, or worse. That's what happened to Gentleman Joe. Went to tell a cop he knew something about a killing and got hisself shot for it.

Breath catching her throat, she turned around to see a police car turning down State Street north of Lake. She felt the silvery headlights of the car staring her down as it rolled quietly forward. Imagined blue lights spinning in a way that most certainly did not say Christmas.

She had to get out of here.

Across the street. To the L-Train, maybe.

Yes, that was it. She knew how to disappear in foot traffic.

Johnny had to pull a bum outta the trash bin, but he was mad as hell and it felt good to have someone to kick around a little. It was nearing lunchtime, and he'd already missed Victoria's coffee and eggs for this shit. From the sound of her voice when he called to say he was still working, he'd be missing the roll, too.

"But it's Christmas, Johnny!" she said, as if that made a difference to Arty.

"I know, sugar. I'll be in as soon as I can."

"Are you seeing something on the side?"

He denied it, of course. And it was true. True enough, anyway.

His problem today, though, was that Arty Cametti wasn't someone who could be fucked with anymore, and it was damned clear the boss was stressed over the missing phone. All Johnny knew for sure was that the woman he'd taken to the basement had to have pulled something over him, had to have figured something was going to go down when he stopped her, and had to have hidden the phone somehow.

It was enough for him to get a good anger worked up, which made finding the bum buried half-inside the garbage dump with his ass up in the air so fortunate.

"You find a phone in there, old man?" he screamed at the bum as he kicked him again. The pounding of his foot against the man's ribs brought a certain sense of justice to him. Johnny was good at his job. Not his fucking fault if the guy was sticking his nose in places it didn't belong. "You find it?"

"No," the miserable fuck of a man groaned, all curled up on the cracked concrete.

Johnny pulled the guy up by his collar. It wasn't hard work. Johnny was a big man, and the guy was skinny under the Army parka. His bones might already be broken. Blood ran down a fold of the bum's mouth.

The act of frisking him was almost as disgusting as the idea of doing the dumpster diving himself. No phone, though. The guy was telling the truth. Johnny looked at the dumpster.

"It's your lucky day, friend. You're gonna go back in there and show me a phone, got it? If you're good, maybe I give you a present."

It took thirty cold as fuck minutes to be certain that the dumpster was lacking anything that resembled a phone.

"Maybe Bobo's got it," the bum said.

"Bobo?" Johnny replied.

She should have tossed the phone into a garbage can as she went, but when she tried, the memory of the girls in the picture welled up and stopped her.

"Not happening," she said to herself.

She wasn't throwing the girls away.

With the phone in her pocket and the ominous image of the cop car in her mind, the idea of sitting in the open scared Bobo. So rather than work, she went to her nook—which was a tight place where two brick walls came together to give shelter from the wind, and was small enough she could cram the duffle bag down to block one direction and use a folded chunk of cardboard to close off the above and the other. Together, it was a space that caught the warmth of her body.

"Ain't much," she'd said to Boomer one day when he asked to see it, "but it's homey enough."

He'd whistled and grinned and thanked her for showing off how she'd used an old blue marker to make a picture of the sky up high on the brick wall.

Bobo appreciated that.

Rain had smeared it to nothing but a big blotch now, but she'd be able to remember it as sky, and she'd also be able to remember the tone of Boomer's voice when he looked at her work. This was her safe place. The place she felt like she belonged.

She hadn't seen Boomer in at least a week, though.

Bad, she thought, as she tucked herself in.

Very bad.

Once she was settled, Bobo pushed the button to turn on the phone.

The screen glowed blue, and she was suddenly sad.

Bobo still wanted to get the phone back to the woman, but there was nothing to do for it. The woman was gone missing, and Bobo knew what it meant for someone to be gone missing.

She wished she could do something.

The icon for the phone caught her eye, though. It felt familiar to her—the shape of the phone—ear part and talking part spanned by the handle. It reminded her of when they had one. That was a long time ago. It had been big and clunky with thick pushy buttons.

It might be nice to call the mayor and complain about the dogs, she thought.

Sister Fred said that life would be a lot better if the dogs were off the street, and Bobo was inclined to agree with him.

She pushed the phone button and was delighted when a number pad came up.

She pushed some, smiling as the phone chirped and beeped with each number.

She put the phone to her ear.

"Hello?" she said.

Nothing.

She pushed a few more buttons, pausing when she heard an odd ringing.

"Hello," she said, holding it to her ear again, then waiting as it rang two more times before a female voice came over the line.

"Hello, you've reached Travis Insurance, how may I help you?"

Bobo found herself unable to respond.

"Hello?" the voice said again.

"Who is this?" Bobo replied.

"I'm Kelly Mendez, how may I help you?"

"Can I talk to the mayor?"

"Excuse me?"

"I want to have a word about the dogs."

"I think you have the wrong number, sir."

Bobo snorted. Sir. No one had ever called her sir before.

After another moment of silence, the woman's voice came again. "Thank you for calling Travis Insurance." Then the phone went silent.

Bobo's first sensation was one of loneliness.

She was used to being by herself. But just a moment before she had been actually talking to someone she didn't even know, and that someone had called her sir, which was funny and which made her somehow happy in a way she couldn't explain.

She wanted to talk to Kelly Mendez again.

I'll do better this time, she thought as she pushed the buttons. *I'll say hello and ask how her day is going.*

The phone eventually rang again.

"Hello?" a young voice came this time. A boy. Maybe a teen.

"Is this Kelly Mendez?" Bobo said, confused.

"No."

"Is this the mayor?"

The young man laughed. "That's funny," he said. "Who is this?"

"I'm Bobo."

"I think you've got the wrong number, Bobo. But Merry Christmas anyway."

"Merry Christmas to you, too," she said.

Then the phone went dead.

Bobo smiled to herself. She had enjoyed the sound of the young man's voice. The playful way he said Merry Christmas reminded her of how she'd felt on the way to the phone store. The dim shadow of her nook felt warmer around her.

She cleared her head and dialed again.

"Merry Christmas!" she said this time when the answer came.

"Merry Christmas!" the response came back.

Over the next several minutes she talked to more people, and while none of them were Kelly Mendez or the mayor most seemed happy to talk to her. Some told her to have a Happy Holiday, others wished her a great New Year. One woman was shopping. "What should I get my boyfriend?" she asked. Bobo thought of Sister Fred. "A good pair of socks is hard to beat," she replied. The woman laughed. "That's great," she said.

Bobo put her head against the bricks after that one. She liked thinking about a man getting a good pair of socks. She pretended she was going to have coffee with the woman tomorrow, and they'd sit like friends and she'd hear about the woman's man. Maybe Bobo would pretend Sister Fred was her man, just to have something to share.

The next call was a young woman. Another teen, maybe a little younger.

"Merry Christmas," Bobo said.

"Yeah," the girl responded.

The phone was quiet for too long. Then the girl sighed.

"I hope you have a good day," Bobo added.

"It'll be good enough, I guess. I'll be going to grandma's."

"That sounds wonderful."

"I'd rather stay home and work on my website. I'm trying to make a private place where only me and my friends can get into."

"I like that," Bobo replied. "It sounds like Heaven."

"The protocol system is all screwed up though. Or something. I don't know. I mean, nothing ever works out right, does it?"

Bobo didn't know what to say, but the girl didn't hang up.

"At least it's something to take my mind off stuff."

"I see."

"What's your name," the girl asked.

"Bobo."

"I'm Quinn."

"Hello, Quinn."

Bobo waited, but while she could hear Quinn rustling around, the girl didn't say anything. "Are you okay?" Bobo finally said.

"Yeah," Quinn replied. "I guess I am."

Time passed, but Quinn still didn't say anything. Bobo waited because her tongue didn't have anything to add, but as the seconds ticked away she felt her muscles tense up and a ball form up inside her throat. There *was* something wrong.

"I'm just worried about my dad." The girl cleared her throat, then breathed again. "My God, this is silly, who are you again?"

"I'm Bobo, what's wrong with your daddy?"

"He's in Afghanistan," she said.

Bobo didn't know where that was.

"Everyone's going to be together tonight, you see. And they'll talk about all this shit that doesn't matter." She gave an awkward pause. "Is it okay if I cuss with you?"

"You can do whatever you want."

Quinn started to cry.

"But no one's going to say the things they're thinking."

"What are they thinking?"

"That he's not coming home."

"I see," Bobo said. "What about your momma?"

"She left us last year."

"So if your daddy doesn't come home, you'll be alone."

The phone rustled, and Bobo knew Quinn had wiped her nose. "Yes," the girl's voice came through in a thin stream.

"My daddy killed my Momma."

"Jesus," Quinn said. "What happened?"

"She didn't cut the carrots right."

"I'm sorry to hear that."

Bobo drew in a deep breath and held it. She didn't like to visit this part of her life. Didn't like to remember it. But she was talking to Quinn, and the words just came out.

"Is your daddy a good man?" she asked.

"Yes. He's smart, and brave, too." Quinn's laugh was pure, then. "When I was little, he used to swing me upside down. And he'd fly me like an airplane in the sky, calling me out like I was a pilot."

Quinn took in a breath.

"He's a great dad."

"Then when he does get back, give him a hug for me."

"A hug from Bobo," Quinn said. "I will."

"Barbara," Bobo replied without thinking. "Everyone calls me Bobo now, but my real name is Barbara."

"All right," Quin said.

They were quiet for a moment too long.

"Where do you live, Barbara?"

The question stopped her. She looked at the wall in front of her, and the duffle, and her cardboard.

"I can't say," Bobo replied. "I got to go now. Merry Christmas, all right?"

"All right," Quinn said. "Thank you, Barbara. Merry Christmas."

After a break, Bobo talked to a lady in Colorado who was baking a pumpkin pie. Then a college kid who said she was Jewish, so she didn't do Christmas. "I didn't know there was anyone like that," Bobo said. The woman taught her how to say Hanukkah. "I like how that sounds in my mouth," Bobo told her. "Me too," she replied. Then the girl wished her a Merry Christmas.

A trucker named Dejuan was still on the road because "you gotta make a buck, even on Christmas Eve." He'd been late delivering refrigerators to a place, but now he was heading home and talking to a stuffed animal he'd bought for his boy sitting co-pilot with him to help him keep awake.

"You sound like a wonderful father."

He got quiet for long enough that Bobo thought she'd lost him.

"I try," he said. "That's gotta count for something."

"Well, Merry Christmas," she said.

"Merry Christmas to you, Bobo. You seem like a real nice lady."

When she was finished with Dejuan, the phone popped up with a note about the battery.

Bobo held the device in both hands, not knowing how much longer she had.

It was late now.

Her self-made cubby was dark in evening shadows, but her gaze went to the blotted spot where she'd colored in the sky, and she remembered Boomer's voice and the way his eyes danced. She thought of the voices on the phone today, and her chest welled up with such a force that for the first time in a long time, Bobo found herself crying.

Not with pain or sorrow or loneliness, but with happiness that she couldn't explain.

The world was beautiful.

As the night got darker, she dialed again.

Johnny pulled his collar up as he stepped into the alley that the second bum directed him to. The sky was already growing dark. This time of year sucked for that. Pitch black by 6:30. With luck, he'd be home by then. Victoria was gonna be pissed off no matter what, but if he wasn't home in time for dinner there'd be real hell to pay.

He'd have been earlier, but Donny Freeman, the guy doing his phone work, wasn't answering, and it took half a day to find the second bum. He was gonna bust Donny up good next time he saw the geeker. A man's gotta work when the customer says to work.

The alleyway was small and twisted, just large enough at the front that a truck could back in for the garbage—a pizza place on one side and a steak place on the other. Not bad if you gotta eat from the bins, he supposed. You could do worse. The buildings were red brick that looked like they'd been built back in the thirties. A tree was growing in a patch of dirt out front of the pizza place, but there was nothing but concrete in the back. Thick pipes ran down the walls. Crates lay in a pile behind the pizza place, and garbage bins stood on both sides of the alleyway. A Mexican place was further down the way.

He snuffled, and hoped he wasn't getting a fucking cold.

A muffled voice came from down the alley, then a pause, then another piece of conversation. A phone call, coming from underneath the dirty piece of cardboard that lay across a small opening that led further down the alley.

Johnny smiled like a tiger as he ripped the cardboard aside to find a dirty shell of a woman hunched over against the wall, talking into a phone.

"Bobo?" he said, enjoying the feel of the smile stretching across his face.

Bobo looked up.

It was dark in the shadows, but the man loomed overhead even darker. Huge, with a belly and arms to match. He wore a black leather jacket, the collar up around his throat.

She clutched the phone just as the man's hand crushed her shoulder.

He lifted her like he was a human crane.

"Hello?" the voice came from the phone. *"Are you still there?"*

The man pinned Bobo against the wall with one forearm, and ripped at the phone with his free hand.

Bobo yanked it away. "It's mine," she said, struggling against the pain of the man's weight against her chest. He leaned in harder, and she thought the point of his elbow was going to split her in two.

His breath smelled worse than the garbage she'd fished the

phone out of.

This close, his cheeks were pockmarked and fleshy.

"Give me the goddamned phone," he wheezed.

"No," she replied, using the last of her willpower to pull his head toward her.

She bit him then, her teeth ripping into the flesh of his ear, the motion of her head pulling away.

He screamed and stepped back.

She fell to the ground, knees buckling, her side crashing to the asphalt so hard it took her breath.

"Bobo?"

The phone was still in her hand. It was a friend, a voice on the other end. She couldn't let go.

"Give me the goddamned phone," the man said again.

He held his hand to the side of his face, blood glistening black through his fingers as he kicked her.

Pain exploded across her back.

Bobo tried to scream, but nothing came out.

He kicked her again.

The man was going to kill her right here on this Christmas Eve, just like daddy had done Momma on the Christmas Eve when Bobo was eight. He was going to beat her until her teeth were gone and until blood ran over her face and into her pretty hair.

A bright light flooded the alleyway and, for a moment, Bobo thought she was being visited by angels.

Then she saw it was not one light, but two.

Headlights. White. And blue. Flashing.

The police.

Bad.

Bad, bad, bad.

She tried to crawl, but she couldn't move.

The man cursed and turned around.

"That's enough," a voice called from some ethereal place Bobo couldn't claim to know. "Stand with your hands up."

Then the cops had the man in handcuffs, and one was helping her sit up.

"Are you all right?" the officer said. It was a man. He smelled like coffee. "Do I need to get you to a hospital?"

Bobo could finally breathe.

She twisted her body around and didn't think anything was broken.

She nodded. "I'm fine," she said. "How did ... why are you here?"

The cop smiled. "You've got a friend somewhere."

Bobo stared at him. "What do you mean."

"All I can say for sure is a kid traced one of your calls. Said you were using Angela Petty's phone. She had it all—your number and its GPS—so it was easy enough to find you then."

"Quinn," Bobo said under her breath.

She coughed against the cold alley, wanting to get back into her nook.

"In the meantime," the cop said, "I'd like to see what's on that phone of yours. If we're right, you might be able to save a young lady's life."

When confronted with the depth of his situation, Johnny "Two Bones" Bracca began to sing. "Your boss is going to prison for a very long time, Johnny," the detective told him. "So how about you start making things better for yourself by telling us where Angela Petty is."

An hour later, the woman was rescued.

Two hours after that, Angela Petty was home with her girls, arriving on her doorstep just before midnight.

Bobo knew this because she was standing outside the television station when the news broke, watching the broadcast from the street as the woman was escorted up her front steps. She saw the girls open the door. Watched as they hugged each other.

The big man was going to be arrested, but that didn't matter to Bobo much.

Instead, she thought about Quinn, and Dejuan, and the other people she'd spoken with. The phone was gone, but their voices were still stuck inside her head.

She had friends out there.

Somewhere.

At least someone who cared enough to help her.

When the news broadcast was finished, Bobo left the station.

It was a long walk to her nook. The streets were empty now, or at least as empty as streets got in Chicago. She was hungry again, but there was something about the moment that made her feel strong anyway. She felt the city in a way she hadn't felt it before.

"Hey?" a voice called as she passed the donut shop.

It was a man standing in the open doorway, holding a small cardboard box full of donuts in one hand.

"You want these?" he called out. "We're finally closing up and I'm just gonna dump them out anyway."

"Thank you," she said as she tucked them under her arm. "Merry Christmas."

"Merry Christmas," he replied.

As she walked on, she came to a place where an underground system blew hot air into the night. She paused there to reach into the box, letting the warm blast prickle her toes while she lifted a donut to her nose first, then took a bite.

It began to snow, then.

Just a few silver flakes swirling like fairies in the street lights.

It was going to be a cold night, but for that minute Bobo Kennedy felt good.

I was in a mood when I wrote "Hero #8" for Kerrie Hughes's _Fiction River: Taverns_ volume. I want to say I'd just seen the Ken Burns documentary on Vietnam—though to be honest, it could have been something else. I was thinking about heroes when the prompt came, and about what we—as society—do to the people we send to war, how the kids we send _never_ come back, how even when they survive physically they all are changed into something they weren't before.

That made this a hard story to write. There were things I wanted to say, and to say them I had to get my mind into places that were more than a bit uncomfortable. Such is life. Truth can be hard.

Hero #8

This is a story about faith.

It begins with a table at lunchtime: small enough for two, square and sturdy, made of blond wood that's been sanded and polished. It has a single, solid base, and sits in McCaffrey's, which is well-lit as far as bars go. A black #8 is printed on one of those plastic cards you get after you order something and you're waiting for a server to bring your food. The card is jammed into a wire-frame holder that's been painted green.

"Who are you?" the woman across from me says as she settles into her chair.

The place smells of dark coffee, strawberries, and white wine.

It's as noisy as you would expect of a place with twelve conversations happening at the same time, and with chairs screeching against tiled floor after the transitions. The background music is a cover of "Walking on Sunshine" being played in *bossa nova* style and sung by a breathy-voiced chick who sounds massively French, which is all very strange for McCaffrey's.

This is the closest thing this little town has to a firefighter bar.

The walls are filled with old patches and photos of trucks and hose beds, guys in gear, and black-and-whites of old fires. Memorabilia sits everywhere, peeling helmets and dented buckets rusted from the years. The hallway to the john is painted with a star for every firefighter in town. You get one the minute you join the house. I got mine three years ago. McCaffrey's is a safe place, it's open to the public, but Ken and Lizzie take care of us—they keep it sane and make sure we have our space when it's clear we need it. The pool table in the back is there just for us.

Ken and Lizzie understand.

"I'm just a guy," I reply to the woman with a sly smile that's worked before.

The facts are that I'm a firefighter and I'm here on a charity auction: "Speed Date a Hero for the Kids," they call it. But she already knows that much. If things work out, she'll pay her hundred bucks or whatever, and we'll go on a date. If not, she'll pay for some other guy from the house and they'll do it. Or maybe she'll do the humane thing and just donate the cash and we can both go on with our own business. What she doesn't know is that most of us are only here because the mayor practically begged us to do it (it's true that a firefighter can pretty much pull a girl any night of the week, and I really do have better things to do than sit here doing lunch in my slacks and sport jacket). She doesn't know that I'm thirty-three and long-time divorced, or that I turned two tours in Iraq, or that I'm trying to figure out how I'm going to pay my rent next week if the job at the store falls through. Maybe construction, I think. I could do that.

"My name is Devin," I say. "Devin Hamilton."

She smiles. "I'm Miranda Moss."

I'm guessing thirty-four, maybe thirty-five years old. Different from your run-of-the-mill badge bunny: 5'6", 130, dark hair, dark skin, very professional. Her sleeveless dress is dark and conservative, but it exposes toned shoulders and biceps with definition. The entire package says she works out, but her desk job keeps her inside all day. Her purse is a soft leather handbag big enough for her phone, some credit cards, and if stereotypes are to be believed, keys and makeup and tissues and a first-aid kit and just about anything else she might need. Its clasp is gold. She leaves it casually on the table.

In other words, everything about her screams "out of my league."

"What do you do?" I ask.

"I, um," she says, "I manage customer accounts for a Fortune 500 company."

"Ah," I reply. "A corporate animal."

"My reputation precedes me."

I catch the fatigue in her tone. "It's that bad?"

"Only if you believe my mother."

"Well, *my* mother thinks I shouldn't run into fires."

"*Your* mother is probably right."

"And yours isn't?"

The daggers in her expression could maim.

"Sorry," I say.

I glance at the clock and see we've already used one of our five minutes.

"If I bid on you, where will we go?"

Miranda is the ninth woman I've talked to, but the first to ask that question up front. Most lead with something about wondering what it's like to run into a fire, some ask if I've saved anyone. One breaks the mold, leans in close, and asks if I would fetch her cat if it ran up a tree, though she uses a different word than "cat." But eventually they all get around to asking where I'll take them. I almost give Miranda the same answer I gave the others: Dinner and a movie, with maybe some drinks afterward if she was up for it. But I stop myself this time.

"Maybe we start with a tour of the station?"

She raises her eyebrows.

"Are you allowed to do that?"

"Why not?"

"None of the other guys have made that offer."

I glance around the bar where eleven of my ladder brothers are busy regaling eleven other women in an attempt to wring the most cash from them. Unknown to the women, we've all chipped 50 bucks into a pool—the guy who gets the biggest bid gets half, the rest goes to the kids, too.

"Maybe they think you'd see it as boring."

"And you don't?"

"Well," I shrug. "I like it."

"What do you like about it?" Her expression is open now, it shows real interest. Her simple intimacy makes me uncomfortable, but I like her voice. Her voice is calm, and it feels good to talk to her.

"It's home, I guess."

She nods. "That's how I feel about the office. I know how it works."

"Yes. That's what I mean."

"But," she says as she sits back in the chair, "lately I've found myself thinking there really ought to be more to life than a glass-walled office with a view."

For a moment I'm surprised that her comment makes me angry, then I realize why. This is why she's here. She's a corporate bigwig slumming with the common folk, dropping a wad of cash on some faceless kids to appease her guilt, maybe take a selfie with a firefighter to put on her Facebook page. She's probably getting props from her company for coming here today.

I hope my smile isn't too ironic.

"Yeah," I say. "It always seems like there should be something more."

Miranda takes a close-lipped breath, holds it, then exhales quickly.

"A tour does sound interesting, though," she says.

I look at her, and wonder if I'm wrong.

This is the moment when there is a disturbance outside.

Tires squeal and a horn blares. The sound of impact is as deep as an ocean, hard and thick, metal-on-metal. You hear it once and you never forget it. Glass and shrapnel clatter over concrete like a wave prattling up the shore.

By the time the yelling and the screaming starts, I'm already out the door.

My brain clicks and things begin to register.

SUV in the middle of the intersection blazing metallic red in the midday sun. Front end gone. Ran a light and plowed a Jeep. The horn is still blaring. The SUV's engine is dead, but the Jeep is still running. I pull a kid away from the scene, and I see he was just standing there, filming with his phone.

"Call 911!" I yell.

It's hot out, and I'm already sweating. I strip off my sport jacket and get to work.

The SUV has passengers. The Jeep is just one guy. It's not pretty. By now the rest of the guys are catching up to me. Three of them split off to manage traffic, and the rest secure the area. The street smells like fuel and burned rubber. Liquid drips to the asphalt and waves of heat ripple from the van.

We get the guy in the Jeep off his horn and now a country song is playing about a girl and a pickup truck. Panicked voices leak through my shell.

I go to the SUV on the passenger's side.

The front of the van is crushed and the wind screen is shattered into a frosted sheet. It's very, very bad. My gaze locks onto the bullet hole on the driver's side. I glance up to a building across the corner. Fourth-floor window is open.

Another crack comes.

Petey McGuire, who was working to get the driver out, goes down.

People scream now. Footsteps pound on pavement.

I swing the SUV's passenger door open and squat down to take cover in the wedge between it and the vehicle itself.

The driver is a woman, youngish, probably Puerto Rican. Part of her forehead is gone and her seat belt is the only reason she's still sitting. Blood is everywhere, and more facts lock in. The accident happened when she was shot and her foot reacted.

I glance up to the darkened fourth-floor window to see the barrel of a rifle. It has a ridged front sight. Probably bolt action.

The woman in the passenger seat keeps asking about Clarissa, who I assume is the driver. I tell her not to worry, but I see the glaze of shock already covering her face. I need to get her out of here, but the front of the car is pushed in over her. I reach down to feel around and know she's trapped—worse, the entire front panel has done deep damage across both her legs. A river of blood is already spilling down to the asphalt at my feet. Her skin is already paling out.

"Can you hear me, ma'am?" I say. "Can you move?"

Another shot comes.

"My girls?" she mumbles. Her right eye opens, and she gasps. She tries to turn to the back, but can't get her arms to move. "My girls?"

Two kids are in car seats in the back. Ace Marek is already unbuckling them. They look more scared than hurt. A moment later, they're out of the car and he's running down the sidewalk with one hooked under each arm.

The shooter is either reloading, or just decides not to take them.

"It's all right, ma'am," I say, hearing the steady tone to my voice.

But it's not going to be all right.

This is a newer model car. The front end is not coming off without hydraulics, and the flow of blood hitting the bottom of the car combined with the feel of her skin is enough to tell me she's going to bleed out before the medics get here.

I hold her hand.

She tries to talk but her words just become a pain-filled moan.

For a minute I don't hear country music or the sound of the Jeep's engine. For a minute I ignore the shooter overhead and just hold her hand tight and talk to her like I've talked to guys before. "You're gonna be comfortable soon, ma'am," I tell her because I know that's as true as I can get. "It's only gonna hurt for a little while longer. Your girls are fine," I say. "Your girls are just fine."

Her eyes close and I keep talking to her.

"My girls," she says one more time.

Then she's gone.

I let go of her hand and glance back to the window, heart pounding, eyes wide.

This doesn't happen here, I think.

Under the smells and sounds of the street, I catch a hint of soup and wings from the restaurant across the way, and flowers from the boutique on the corner.

This doesn't fucking happen here.

It's twenty meters across the street from the SUV to the wall at the corner away from the shooter. If I can get there, I can make a clean run on the building.

A car has been parked at the light this whole time. I see the passenger panic and swing the door open so she can get out.

"Get back in the car!" I scream.

She doesn't listen. The rifle kicks again, and she goes down. Clean shot to the head.

Fuck.

Three shots, three kills. He's a pro. Probably military.

I take advantage of his distraction to make my jump, run to the wall and press up against brick that's hot from the sun. It makes me think of the desert. I smell sand. The absence of a radio voice in my ear makes me feel naked. The brick is gritty and harsh like the broken concrete in bombed-out streets. I taste that same dirt, even though the desert is a long way away. I never thought I would miss the feel of a Kevlar jacket wrapped around me.

The building the shooter is holed up in was once a bank, but now is a set of offices that sell insurance and legal services.

I'm across the street and positioned so that he can't see me unless he either puts his head out the window—which I already know he won't do, or unless he moves to this side of the room he's in—which he might do at any time. I could run now—I could go the other way and let the cops and the SWAT team deal with it. But it's going to take them time to get here, and if someone doesn't stop this guy he's going to kill anyone who moves.

If that happens, I know I won't sleep again for a week.

That's how it is for me.

I don't dream. I don't see rivers of blood streaming out of faucets or hallucinations of battlefields in the dark of nights like all those goddamned commercials that the Armed Forces Network used to run. My burden is sleepless nights and my own voice echoing out my gourd. My luggage is the dull ringing at the top of my skull that never goes away, the feeling that I should have been able to do something more when everyone in their right fucking mind would know that there was nothing left to do. My pain is weighed in its lack of understanding anything anymore and my penalty is sitting up late at night and staring mindlessly at a TV screen or an Internet browser and pretending that there's some reason I'm here.

So, no, running away is not an option for me.

On the other hand, while I know I can get into the building, I'm not a complete and total idiot.

I need a weapon.

Another shot rings out.

I edge to the corner, then hunch down and sprint to the other side of the street. There's a bakery in the next office and a deli beside that. A men's clothing shop is next, and a used book store. Finally there's a sporting goods place.

The glass door's locked.

Smart folks.

I grab a big trash can that's just down the street, and throw it through the glass. The security alarm blares. I go directly to the rack of bats. I forego the aluminum softball bats to grab a hefty piece of wood. Thirty-four inches of polished ash with Mike Trout's signature burned into the barrel.

Then I'm back on the street and slinking toward the insurance building.

In the distance, I hear police sirens.

The streets are emptying, but another car drives up, and the rifle coughs again. The windshield breaks with a single hole that spiderwebs across the glass surface.

I push the door open, and go into the building.

As I make it up the stairwell, I conclude he picked lunchtime on purpose.

The man has a plan.

He didn't want to shoot anything until he got himself set up in the unoccupied corner spaces, and lunchtime, when the offices were least staffed, gave him the greatest chance to make it to his destination point.

He probably chose this building on purpose, too. Its architecture is older. Its stairs go straight up from the main lobby, which means no real foot traffic.

The few offices I pass are already empty, and I see no signs of struggle.

The stairs are old hardwood. They creak as I climb. So much for having surprise on my side.

Another shot rings out as I approach the fourth floor.

The shooter's voice grumbles. "You can't make me do it no more," he says.

No one responds.

The bat is firm in my hand. The air is conditioned too far, and chilled goosebumps cover the back of my neck as the unit kicks in and a column of air moves down the passage.

I stop before coming to the top floor. The stairs whine again. Outside, the sirens draw closer.

"You coming up?" the shooter calls out. "I ain't deaf. I know you're there."

The more he talks the less he shoots.

"Why should I come up there if you're just gonna shoot me?" I call out.

"But that's why you're here, right? Only a jackass wanting to get shot comes up on a man he knows got a gun."

"I been called worse than a jackass."

The shooter laughs. His voice is gruff.

The sound of a round being loaded echoes from the empty office space.

"Look at that asshole getting outta his car," the shooter says. Then he shoots and the magazine loads again.

Why are you doing this? I think. I almost say it, but at the last moment I know better.

"I know how you feel," I say.

"Fuck you."

"How many tours?"

Sirens grow louder.

The ventilation system shuts off and the smell of fresh air edges back into the area. I twist the bat to get rid of anxiety, not that it works. I'm sweating, but my palms are dry. I remember this feeling. Every part of my body wired, eyes wide but not wide enough, ears pinned back, listening. The sense of smell so intense you don't think you can ever breathe out.

"How many?" I ask again.

"Three."

"Sucks."

"Ah," he says. "You get used to it."

"That's right. I know you do. That's the problem, isn't it?"

"Don't go all shrink on me, now."

I shut up.

"How many for you?" he says.

"Two. Both Iraq."

"I got you beat by one Afghanistan."

"You do get used to it, don't you," I say, talking as much to myself as I do to the shooter. "The pressure? The constant code yellow? It's not the firefights that get to you. Not bullets flying close by or even seeing your best friends get all shot to shit. It's the never-ending thing of being on edge twenty-four hours a day. You can't stand down, you know? That's the shit that no one understands. You go in thinking the world is one way, but it all comes out different."

He doesn't have to tell me I'm right.

During the Vietnam War there was a battle over a hill that, like all the other hills in Vietnam, had been given a number. The number itself no longer matters except to the guys who were there, and maybe to a few historians who care about such things.

Before the siege, the hill was lush with multi-layered green forest and elephant grass as tall as a man. Ten days later it was a desolate landscape of mud, bomb craters, and blasted trees.

After the battle, the victorious soldiers gave the hill a name, which one man then put on a sign and bayoneted to a dead tree. Another soldier added a slug line.

Was it worth it? the second note read.

Two weeks later, as happened often throughout that war, the victorious side abandoned the hill and the losing side took it back. It was as if the battle had never happened. Yet, the hill still carries the name the soldiers gave it, and people have written books and movies about it.

Some say that hill changed the war.

Yet, after all these years, the question remains: *Was it worth it?*

"Can I come up?" I say. My voice is calm again, steady like it was when I spoke to the woman who just bled out in her friend's car.

"Still a free country last I checked."

"I don't want to get shot."

"You pays your money, you takes your chances."

I swallow, take a bracing breath, and nod to myself.

The stairs creak as I climb them.

He's not a big man: about my size, but thin, and with corded muscles. He's clean-shaven. His light-colored hair is freshly cut in a military buzz, probably sandy blonde when it grows out. He's sitting on a simple hard-backed chair in a wide office with the window open. The chair is far enough from the window that no one is going to be able to get a shot at him from the ground.

The rifle is across his lap.

He's got a handgun strapped to his belt. Full-sized Glock, model 21 .45 ACP. One of the classic big boys.

He wears fatigue pants and boots. A standard tan T-shirt shows under his unbuttoned camo shirt. A Velcro tag with the name "Joyce" is stuck on the right side of the shirt. His gaze slips between me and the window.

"Nice baseball bat," he replies.

"Mike Trout."

"Helluva hitter."

I motion to the barren Velcro patches on the left of his shirt. "You're not flying your unit."

"This ain't about them."

"What's it about?"

He lifts the Glock from his holster.

"You're the one said you understood."

"I understand that whatever you're feeling right now is your own, and that you're the one who has to come to grips with it."

"That's bullshit."

Joyce points the Glock out the window, but doesn't shoot. I understand the mindset of a sniper. The handgun's not going hit anyone but me from this distance.

"You don't have to do this alone," I say.

He smiles, and his eyes flare with an edgy brightness. The Glock waves like a conductor's baton as he talks.

"All these people think there's a reason for this shit, don't they? They pretend the world cares about them—work your ass off, they all say, and something good happens. They think there's God or a hero, or even just a simple goddamned plan someplace that says if you're good, if you're really just fucking good, that's enough. But they don't know the truth, do they? They all pretend they fucking matter. They think they make a goddamned difference."

He stops and shrugs.

The sirens arrive.

I need to get hold of that gun. I see it now. I know where he's planning to go with this, and it's suddenly deeply important that I get hold of that gun.

I step toward him, hand out.

He points the Glock my way, and I stop.

"Come downstairs with me."

"No," he says. "I don' t think that's how I'll be doing this."

Then Sergeant Fred Joyce of the Army Sniper Corps and veteran of three tours in service of his country puts his gun to his head and ends the standoff himself.

I call 911 from the empty office.

I sit with Joyce until the cops come, staring at his body, seeing the blood run as red as mine would run if I were in his shoes. For the next hour the police go over every detail with me, then tell me I can leave. They'll be cleaning up the site for hours.

I go back to McCaffrey's.

Speed Date a Hero is over, of course.

The twelve women have all gone, some writing checks anyway. I wonder whether Miranda paid and, if so, how much. I think about her sitting in her office: that safe place where she knows how things work. I imagine her pecking at a computer with her shoes off underneath her desk.

Someone on the street picked my jacket up and turned it in. Cindy Maroni, the daytime manager at the bar, gives it to me. Captain Moore claps me on the shoulder and puts his other hand on my arm. "You did good today, Devin. Go home. We'll cover your shift."

"I'll go back to the station," I say.

I want to be there now. I want its sense of order: the duty roster, the training regimen, the way that everything has its place so that whenever it's needed that thing is always just there.

"Seriously, Devin," the captain says. "Take the time. You earned it."

I don't want to, but I nod and go back to my car.

Where I sit with the windows rolled up until it gets so hot I can't hardly breathe. Then I start the car and drive down to the river, where I sit on a grassy river bank and watch as the current flows downstream and the birds fly overhead.

All the stories that usually bounce off my brain are in full ricochet mode.

Faces flash in my mind: men and women, a kid who was just trying to get a drink of clean water when a mine went off, Master

Sergeant Lavine, who stood up to his command and was busted the next day.

When I was in Iraq we all watched the ads on AFN. They were filled with grim-faced guys who came off the battlefield with their hands shaking and their brains flashing on flame-filled battlefields. Those guys flashed on incoming and on buddies who wouldn't be coming back. Take care of yourself, those clips said. Talk to someone. But mockery is the better part of valor. If we did ever talk, it was to pick the damned things apart.

The pressure cooker was on the other guys, right?

The ones who broke were the ones who ran street ops, the gung-ho brutes who did door-to-door, or snipers who killed from a distance without knowing who was going down. Those were the guys you had to watch out for. Those were the guys who imagined blood coming out their showerheads or woke up drenched in sweat.

Not us.

When you're in a unit, that's just how it is.

You look at the guy on your left and the guy on your right, and everyone just says We're Good, Let's Do It, and you pretend it's all just fine because your hands are rock solid and your dreams haven't turned to crap. We are all A-fucking-okay. But that's not right. We all know it's not right. Or maybe it is. How the hell can you tell?

I sit here until the sun goes down and it gets cool enough that I need to go somewhere else.

It's 8:00 or so when I get back to McCaffrey's.

To say I'm given a hero's welcome is the understatement of the decade. My back gets sore from the pounding it receives. It's a hard house this evening, though. Petey McGuire is dead, but I saved lives. I try to pay for a drink, but my money is like clay. Everyone bends my arm and tells me how fucking-A goddamned proud they are to know me. Someone finds out I haven't eaten and a steak suddenly appears.

I finally beg off and find a quiet place to eat it.

It's the same table I was at earlier this afternoon, only this time it has no number. The steak is a bit over-done, but good. It comes with a baked potato and broccoli.

As I eat I watch the men and women of the firehouse, the few cops scattered among them, and the civvies—the folks who come here just because they serve a great burger and fries. I watch badge bunnies work the room.

This is my place. It holds me up. These are my people.

I think it's true what Fred Joyce said to me earlier.

I think life *is* random.

One day you're driving down the street and then you're dead. Maybe there isn't any meaning to it. Maybe things just happen. But watching these people gives the story a different twist. Random or not, places like McCaffrey's exist because these people make them exist. I look at these people and I see Fred Joyce in each and every one of them. They wouldn't believe that if I told them, but I feel his truth inside them in a way that I will never be free of.

You can't unsee things, after all.

You can't "recover" from the moment you learn that you—the collection of ideas, feelings, and events that is you, the kid who once said he would play wide receiver in the NFL, or the guy who promised to be faithful to a woman until death do us part, or the guy who patrolled in Fallujah—can change, that the person you think you are can go away in an instant. I can't remove the knowledge that there is a Fred Joyce in each and every one of us.

But I have to believe he was wrong, too.

Even if there is no guarantee from the past and no promise of the future, there can still be purpose. The people here are all the proof I need that there are things bigger than the one seemingly meaningless life I own. There is value in what I do, or at least there can be.

I have to believe that.

I wish that, before his life was ruined and before he broke the lives of so many people, Fred Joyce could have felt the wave I feel underneath me tonight. I wish we were here together a night ago so I could buy him a steak and tell him how goddamned proud I was of his service and that there are things he can do that still make a difference.

I wish I could have helped him hold on just one more day.

"So, how much are you worth?"

The voice startles me. I turn around to see Miranda Moss, the woman from earlier, still dressed in her conservative dress.

"Excuse me?" I say.

She gives her handbag a meaningful shake as she sits down across from me. "I came to make my donation. How much should I bid on you?"

"As much as you think the kids are worth, I suppose."

"Touché," she says.

We sit there. I can see she's tired. I've got bloodstains on my pants.

"Are you okay?" she says.

I look at her. She *is* tired. Her eyes are wide and deep. Her face is lined and her hair is falling from its restraints. She is not as young as she once was. But she seems like she actually cares. It makes me wonder what battles she's fighting. It makes me wonder who she is beneath the corporate veneer.

"I think so," I say to her. "I think I'm going to be okay."

Mike Resnick once told me that he enjoyed editing themed anthologies because it was fun to see writers take twists and turns that no one else would take. When Leah Cutter agreed to edit *Fiction River: Stolen* I knew what I was going to write. I do, of course, love me some baseball. And I'd been playing in a weird "Fake Baseball" computer environment for some time. I even had a couple favorite "Fake" players, one who just happened to be one Carlos Garcia, who was a speed-demon on the basepaths. What better to steal than second base, right?

There's more, of course. A lot more. The story surprised me— which is at the root of a good stolen base, too, I suppose. It turned brutal in ways I hadn't anticipated, but in ways that made sense as the character talked to me. Baseball is a beautiful game on the field, but the people who play it are just that. People. And people have to live in the reality of their environments.

Look Safe

It's gotten to where Carlos doesn't feel the ring in his back pocket anymore.

In quiet moments he'll tell you how good it is to be past all that. He'll say it's good to be seventeen and have a job he loves to do and that pays at least enough to eat and live by himself in a one-room flat toward the center of town, toward the Basilica where the proximity to tourists keeps things fairly safe. He'll say there are worse places to be.

But this is neither a quiet moment nor a particularly good one. His team is behind, 2-1. They are "on the road," playing in Punta Cana, which is just far enough away that the team paid for a bus. It's the top of the eighth inning, and he's standing on first base.

Or, to be more precise—which Carlos has always tried to be—he's standing *near* first base.

The lights are just now turning on, and the sky above is gloaming in that startling dark blue that matches the nearby ocean. It's streaked with red clouds and filled with the dark, circling forms of gulls and the occasional hawk or kite that wheel around over the docks. The moon sits on the horizon, half-full. If he thinks about it, the air smells like plantains and motorcycle exhaust—but then that's what the air always smells like here. He hates the smell of plantains because it reminds him of the reek of his father's hands when he would come home about this time every night, dazed on drink and tired from harvesting.

His father was never a kind man, but he was honest.

The crowd is chattering with unhappiness because a moment ago Pasqual Renteria hung a tired slider that Carlos plastered into left for a hit. They want to go home to drink and smoke, or maybe listen to the radio and dance, or just trade stories in the humid darkness of the island. But they also want to win, and this is the Island. They aren't going to leave until the game is finished. So now the old men sit on their bench seats smoking cigars and spitting. Younger men shout out, women whoop and holler. The stands down toward right field are lined by rusted rails wrapped with the fingers of young boys, their eyes bright in the darkness.

Somewhere in the shadows Carlos had been told that a scout from one of the American teams is here specifically to see him. He's tried not to think much about that, but it was damn near impossible.

That's something else about being seventeen and having something that is both a dream and more than a dream. Your emotions get all tangled up until you can't think straight. And Carlos likes to think straight. He knows exactly what he's got on the line, but he likes to focus on the job at hand. It's something he's good at.

His team is behind 2-1. His manager, a hard-nosed guy everyone knows as Tito, has given him the green light.

Everyone in the rickety little stadium knows he's going to steal.

So he tries his best to ignore the dark outline of the man in the shadows of the bleacher stands that lay along the first base line.

Carlos heard their father come home that night. His footsteps clomped up the stairs with a gait that spoke of too much rum.

The three-room place they rented from the furniture maker below was on one of the hundreds of narrow alleyways that ran through La Florida. The dull roar of chattering voices and boom-box music came through the open window. The street below was half dirt, half cracked concrete that got messy when it rained. And it always rained. The buildings here were squashed flat and built so close enough together that only rats, cats, and the skittery geckos his mother loved so much could make it through the gaps. The brick was painted in peach or aqua that had faded in the sun, red sometimes, occasionally orange, but always peeling. The businesses here were slathered in mud-stained advertisements that were mostly in Spanish, which marked this neighborhood as not a place for tourists, not smart ones anyway. English said there was money to be made here. Spanish was for where people lived.

Their window had a view of the Carmelos' living room, which tonight was filled with laundry and Mrs. Carmelo's chattering.

Carlos had left school early to play baseball in the street that afternoon. He wasn't going to, but Juan told him he should.

"I've got a test," Carlos said, arguing.

"Won't be no one testing off the Island," his brother replied.

They were standing in the open-air corridor of the school.

Carlos was twelve, Juan three years older. He was taller than Carlos, and his arms, scarred with the Diaz brand two years ago, were getting thicker. He wore a black T-shirt that carried the image of Havana G, a Cuban rapper who was hot in certain circles. Sweat from the afternoon heat glistened at the hollow of his throat and dampened the shirt. That shirt and the red baseball cap, perfectly clean with its blazing white logo of the Chicago White Sox, said he was approachable—to a certain clientele. It said he was carrying. In the days when Juan first got into the Diaz gang, Carlos had asked Juan to leave it. Just stay away. A year later when he saw the money that was starting to show up in Juan's pocket, Carlos asked to get him in. Both times Juan had laughed and done nothing. "The streets steal more than they give, Little CG," he said when he asked again.

"I can't miss the test or Mama will rip skin off my behind."

"I'll take it for you," Juan argued. "Teacher won't give no shit."

The idea of playing ball was strong, and Juan was right. All the teacher cared about was getting everyone out of the building come 3:45.

"It's geography, right?" Juan said with that smile of his that was always getting girls' attention these days.

"Yeah."

"You know I got that down."

Carlos hesitated.

"Baseball gonna get you off the island faster than geography, little brother. I see you play. I know what I talking about."

Carlos hesitated.

"Go on." Juan shooed him like a fly.

He was always doing that. Building him up. Telling him he could be someone if he just went to play ball.

It was working, too. Carlos was beginning to think he could do it. Beginning to think he could play the game as well as anyone. Certainly he was already better than the boys his own age, and often better than those older than him. He could cover centerfield like flypaper, and he could already hit a little.

He liked that his big brother was pushing him. Liked that his big brother was paying attention and knew he could play ball. Juan had always been around for him.

Carlos looked at the plastic bag that bulged in his brother's back pocket. "You got a delivery."

"I can make it," Juan said, his smile turning to a frown that reminded Carlos of his father. "Don't worry about me, little CG. Everybody know I'm dependable."

Carlos smiled then. Yes, everybody knew Juan Garcia was dependable.

"You're my best brother ever," he said, already smelling the aroma of the open street where the guys would be playing.

"I'm your only brother."

"And don't you forget it," Carlos said.

A minute later he was outside school grounds.

Later that night, though, when his father came home, Carlos was sitting on the tattered couch and watching a video on his old phone. He was tired and grimy from sweat, but happy. He had hit well, and he could always outrun the others. His mother stood in the kitchen nook preparing the guava and avocado she had bartered for earlier. She planned to fry pork, he remembered that even now because he could recall the aroma of the raw meat laid out on the counter.

A string of motorbikes splattered in the alley, and tinny music played from Mama's radio as his father slammed the door.

The smell of rum and tobacco rolled off him, which wasn't unusual. "Nikki!" he bellowed for Carlos's mother. He was angry about something, which wasn't different, either. Carlos could predict certain parts of the future now. His father would yell at his mother for something. Maybe he would hit her, maybe he wouldn't. The fact that Juan wasn't here was going to make him more upset. His father hated the idea of his boy being in the Diaz gang. He had even tossed Juan out of the house at one point, only letting him come back when Mama threatened to leave.

As his mother appeared at the doorway, another rumbling came from downstairs.

At first Carlos thought it was Juan, just now coming home. The voice was different, though. Higher and angrier.

Then the door burst open behind Carlos's father.

The gunshot was deafening.

Carlos's father lurched forward, then fell to a knee. The next shot took him high in the chest, the next higher. The shooter was angular and thin. His yellow shirt hung off him like a drape. The gun was blacker than the man's skin. Skin marked with the Diaz brand.

The man turned to Carlos's mother.

She was screaming "No! No! No!" and running at him.

The man shot, and she spun around.

Blood.

Carlos would remember the blood for a long time.

He starts with the same lead.

Three steps.

"You don't change nothing," his first coach had told him as he marked the distance with a worn sneaker. "Go or not, you don't give the pitcher no idea what you're thinking."

So that's how Carlos played.

Until he got older, anyway, and saw the way a runner could get into the mind of a pitcher.

He likes that part of the game. Making the other person twist their thoughts up in loops is a special kind of joy he can't get anywhere else but on a ballfield. A lead, he's decided, makes a statement.

Now Carlos starts with those same three steps—but then edges farther, an inch at first, then two or three as time goes on. Despite the time of evening, it's still hot. He can feel himself sweating. He rocks back and forth in his crouch, extending the distance between himself and the safety of first base, then he digs his back cleat into the dirt, listening to the cinders grind as he twists it in.

Renteria is a lefty, which is unfortunate.

With a right-hander you wait for his stretch, then look for movement at the back of the knee to see if he's coming to first or going to the plate. Or you might see how he dips the shoulder, or sometimes the left heel rises just a bit. But a lefty's different. A lefty can cheat the umpire and get away with a balk.

Carlos had learned exactly how lefties can do that from a wrinkled old baseball man one day in the fall. The man was stooped and wore a stained jacket. His skin was dry and wrinkled from years in the sun, and his eyes had that watery flavor that old guys can get. The man had been in the stands while Carlos played and after the game he hunted Carlos down.

They talked about base stealing for a long time, Carlos buying the man a beer to keep him going. His name was Felix. He played in the early days. Slap hitter, second baseman. Said he managed for a bit after his knees got too bad to play. They got along well because the man liked to talk and Carlos liked to listen. The next day Felix came by again. This time he dragged Carlos to the end of the bench, the farthest back spot in the dugout where the angle is closest to actually being on first base. The shadows made that corner dark and cool. Together they watched the pitcher. Each pitch, every inning, all game, Felix whispered to Carlos. "See that?" Felix said, pointing to the twitch of the pitcher's lip. "See that?" he said when the pitcher fell into the pattern of checking over twice before going to the plate. "They do that and you can walk to second."

The next day Felix didn't show up.

Never showed again.

But Felix had changed him. Carlos never saw the game the same way again.

He was a details man, and baseball, it turns out is a details game.

The details that matter now are that his team is down 2-1, and they need him on second base. But there's more here than the team. Carlos feels the scout's eyes on him. Assessing him. Judging him. Carlos's job is to make him like what he sees. Everything that matters to him rides on it.

He edges further off the base.

Despite the fact that Carlos has been studying Renteria all game long, he wants to see this pitcher's movement up close. He wants to see Renteria's pickoff throw.

He gets it, and he's back to first without even a dive.

The first baseman tags him on the thigh, just because he can, then throws the ball back to the pitcher.

It's important to Carlos that he gets back to the base standing—or sideways, Felix called it. Some guys dive all the time, but that just gets you tired. If a pitcher knows you're a diver, he'll throw over three or four times just to make you pick yourself up again and again. There's more to it for Carlos than just staying fresh, though. You get back standing and you tell the pitcher you've got him.

The crowd quiets.

Renteria takes his place on the pitching rubber once again.

If Carlos were the kind of guy who was good in the clubhouse, he would probably be smiling now. There's a wrinkle in the pitcher's white pants that runs just under his left knee. It flattens out when the throw is coming to first. Carlos isn't the kind of guy who's good in a clubhouse, though. People think he's moody, which is a knock on him he's heard from scouts in the past. He doesn't smile a lot. They worry that he's unhappy.

Fuck that, though.

He's happy enough, but he's got business going on.

All Carlos is thinking about right now is that he needs to steal second base.

Then he takes his lead, crouching and rocking back and forth, reading Renteria like he's a book.

<hr>

Carlos froze.

His father lay still on the floor, red blood pooling around him. Mama was writhing and groaning on the woven throw rug that covered part of the floor.

He wanted to run. Yell. Scream. Get the hell off the couch. Go to Mama. He wanted to help her. He wanted to do a million things, but nothing in his entire body would work. The man in the yellow shirt turned the gun to Carlos, and he was finally able to hold his hands up, the stream still playing on the phone.

"Please?" he begged.

Movement came from the doorway.

A black shirt, ragged dungarees. Red hat.

Juan.

His brother's body collided with the shooter, and the two of them fell to the floor, wrestling, tumbling, falling against the bare wood with the sound of clipped elbows and bruised ribs. They yelled over the top of the other. A punch was thrown. Juan pinned the man's gun hand, but the shooter raked his eyes. Juan drove an elbow into the man's chin, drawing more blood. His cap was gone now, scattered somewhere, the dark weave of his hair seemed surreal.

His mother moaned.

The gun shot again, punching a fist-sized hole in the wall. Suddenly the harsh tang of gunpowder was real.

Then Carlos was up from the couch, and grabbing a lamp from the side table.

Juan bit the man's hand.

Both of them kicked at each other. The shooter got his gun hand free, put the gun to Juan's face and pulled the trigger.

In the American leagues, you get 3.2 seconds.

That's it.

The pitcher's delivery to the plate takes 1.3 of that. The time the catcher takes to get the ball to second, if he's a good one, will be 1.9 more—a little less if it's a pitchout. Add them together and the math is clear. Assuming the throw is good, a runner is out if he takes longer than 3.2 seconds to hit the bag, safe if he's quicker.

The gun clicked empty just as Carlos crashed the lamp down on the shooter's head. It shattered with a ceramic crunch. The man was stunned for a moment, but not down.

It was enough, though.

Enough that Juan could get up and swing at him. Kick him. Beat him across the skull, cursing and yelling, pounding on him with everything he had. The man waved his gun at Juan in a feint defense, but Juan was possessed. "I delivered, goddamn it! I delivered!" He grabbed the gun from the shooter and used it to pummel him, screaming the same phrase over and over *Entregué! Entregué! Entregué!*

When Juan was finished, he stood over the shooter's comatose body.

The gun was in his hand, stained red with blood and bits of hair.

Juan's chest heaved. His face glistened with perspiration.

Outside, even the Carmelos' living room seemed to have gone silent.

"Run," Juan said to him.

Carlos stammered, still holding the base of the lamp. Both his father and mother lay in horrific stillness.

"I said run, Carlos," Juan cried. "Now!"

Juan grabbed him by the meat of his shoulder and pushed him out of the room, then down the stairs hard enough that Carlos lost his balance and fell the last half the way. At the bottom, he picked himself up and did what his brother had told him to do. His feet pounded on the dirt-lined street. He was breathing so hard and so fast he nearly choked. There were fewer people in the streets this time of the night, and they were moving in the normal way now. He bounced off a woman. Slid past a man. He was crying now, and the tears made Carlos understand what was happening.

Juan missed a deadline. His parents were dead because Juan missed a deadline, and now Juan was going to find himself in prison.

This was what happens when a Diaz boy misses a deadline. News would travel through the membership. The next boy would not miss.

His parents were dead.

Juan was gone.

Carlos was on his own.

That's what he was thinking as he ran through streets that were beginning to get dark.

He was on his own.

Pasqual Renteria is not a major league pitcher. He might take a tick longer to deliver the ball. And Jorge Gonsalves is not yet a major league catcher—though some are saying the Cardinals are asking after him.

Carlos thinks he has 3.3 seconds this time, maybe a tick more. And Carlos is quicker than the average runner. By his coach's stopwatch he can get to second in just over three seconds. Hence the rumor of scouts.

He should be able to steal this base.

Assuming he gets the read down.

Renteria takes the sign from Gonsalves, and comes set, ball hidden in his glove, fingers working to take his grip. He glances at Carlos, but Carlos isn't falling for it. Renteria gives him a second look.

Carlos takes in the moment.

The sound of the crowd goes away and there is only him and the pitcher.

He dangles his fingers. Breathes in.

Watches.

His eyes catch the wrinkle dissolve, and he launches forward, staying low, crossing his far leg over the front in the way he's practiced thousands of times.

Renteria tries the slide step. It's that quick throw where the pitcher doesn't do a full leg kick, just picks it up and slides it farther ahead to get momentum for the pitch. It's a risky move for a pitcher because, while it speeds up the delivery of his pitch and makes it harder to steal, it takes something away from the pitch itself. That's how life is—tradeoffs everywhere.

The first three steps have to be perfect.

Carlos fights the natural urge to stand up into his launch, stays bent, drives his legs hard to get momentum built as quickly as he can.

Air escapes his diaphragm in a long grunt and his thighs burn.

It was two months before Carlos learned that Juan had, indeed, been put into the prison house.

He went to visit and after four tries was granted ten minutes.

Juan had lost weight here. They sat at a table in the open yard with at least ten men with rifles in the areas Carlos could see. He supposed he should be afraid, but he'd been on his own now for long enough that a gun that wasn't pointed his way wasn't a problem.

It was hot there. Midday on the Island. Everything seemed to be fragile and baking.

Carlos swiped sweat from his brow as a guard escorted Juan.

"Where you at?" Juan said as he sat down. His T-shirt was sleeveless and dirty.

"Where am I living?"

"Yeah."

"Different places."

"Not Mama's?"

"Rented to someone else," Carlos said.

"Stay off the streets, whatever you do," Juan replied.

"I do."

The fact is he's living half in the streets now, and half with families Mama was friends with. It's been long enough that this almost feels normal.

"I'll get you out," he said to his brother when Juan first sat down. "I'll pay."

Juan laughed. "You don't got that kind of cash, man."

"Other gangs than Diaz will pay."

"No," Juan said.

There was power behind that word. One syllable. One note. No. As if there was nothing left to say, but to Carlos there was.

Juan Garcia was in here for drugs and for beating the shooter senseless. But it wouldn't matter really. He was really in for $10,000 US, or $20,000, or whatever the officer of the day thought was enough. And once he'd paid up, he'd be fair game again. Guys got screwed like this every day—paid to get out, then hunted down and put back in for something else the next night. Or maybe worse, hunted down and then just disappeared. But Carlos would pay if he could pay.

"You always looking out for me," Carlos said, choosing his cadence to match Juan's. He'd been on the streets long enough to understand cadence and language. How the tone of a word alone was enough to give you access to a group. Now that he was alone, that was something he understood more about himself. Carlos was good at this kind of thing. Paid attention to details other folks didn't. He liked seeing how things went together. "Now I look after you."

"No," Juan repeated.

"I can get a job."

"No."

"What do you mean, no?"

"I mean I got nothing here, Carlos. Nothing. Get me out I still got nothing. But you, Little CG, you got ball. Go play it. You can do that. You know you can. Everybody knows it. Talk to them if you don't believe me. Go play it, Carlos. Get off the damned Island and don't look back."

Carlos looked at his brother. "I can't leave you in here."

"You can't get me out."

A guard with a rifle slung over his shoulder walked toward the table.

Juan pulled a ring off his pinky finger. It was a simple band of silver.

"Sell it," he said, laying it on the table. "Don't want to see you here again."

Then Juan was gone, and another guard with another rifle slung over his shoulder came for Carlos.

He swept the ring up, and put it on his own finger, thinking hard about what Juan had just told him. Hearing the words of the big brother who had always been there for him telling Carlos there was nothing for him to do.

Juan was right about a lot of things, but about this he was wrong.

If you want to know what stealing a base feels like, hop in your car and get someone to drive you at twenty miles an hour. Then do a belly flop off the hood.

The base comes at Carlos hard.

He dives headfirst because that's faster and he's not certain how good the throw will be. He dives to the outside of the base because it makes the tag longer, and because then it's easier to pop up and get to third on an error.

Hitting the bag stings. The tag comes an instant later.

He doesn't even listen for the umpire's signal, just stands himself up and begins to dust himself off.

"You want to just look safe," Felix told him just before he left that last day. "When you slide in, you don't look to the umpire to see what he's thinking. 'Stead you just make yourself look safe. Just stand there and go to dusting yourself off like nothing happened."

"Jackie Robinson, stealing home," Carlos said.

If you follow baseball, you've seen the picture of Jackie Robinson stealing home.

It was a World Series game. Yogi Berra was catching. Until the day he died, Berra claimed Robinson was out.

"You got it."

Those were the last words Felix said to him.

It turns out the umpire agrees.

When Carlos collects himself, he sees Renteria has deflated. As have the fans. One pitch, one base. They don't know exactly how Carlos Garcia is going to score, but they all know he is going to.

In the stands, American man edges out of the shadows. He has a stopwatch in one hand, a clipboard in the other, and a deeply satisfied smile on his face.

Things settle, and Carlos reaches runs his hand over the pocket where he keeps his brother's ring.

Juan's image comes then, sitting on the prison bench and squinting through a savage sun. The smell of hard-baked dirt comes, the sound of men working. He imagines Juan there, sees his brother swinging a scythe up and down, clearing crap from the fields until he withers up and dies.

Carlos takes a last glace at the American scout, then focuses on the pitcher.

If he works hard enough, he's going to run himself right off the Island.

When he does, he's coming back.

Kris Rusch likes historical fiction. That much I knew. When she said she was looking for stories to fill _Fiction River: Spies_ I immediately jumped to the cold war. I quickly discarded that idea, though, because I thought other people might do it and because, despite an interest of the period, I don't know enough about that kind of spy game to write it to my satisfaction without doing a _lot_ of research first.

So, instead, I thought about Chicago—which is a city I love to be in—and as soon as I thought about Chicago, I knew what I had to write about. Similar to "The White Game" at the front of this volume, "The Spy Who Walked into the Cold" benefited from a suggestion from Kris—or in this case, an admonishment that I'd left out the most important scene. I'll leave it to you to determine which that was, but I'll just note here how happy I am that she took the chance of letting me add it.

The Spy Who Walked into the Cold

I dreamed of the fight in A Shau Valley again.

Three years back and I still saw it clear as day.

It's raining the kind of rain that only falls when you're on your own in an isolated camp out in the middle of the jungle, big drops that pelt your shoulders like bullets and make your helmet drum against your brain. Ten of us Green Berets from the 5th Special Forces and a couple hundred civilian irregulars are there to keep the Viet Cong off the Ho Chi Minh Trail. A couple NVA spooks who came over said they had four battalions in the area and after we asked twice the brass believed it enough to send us a MIKE company and a handful of new Berets, so we know they're coming.

Everyone understands Charlie needs to clear the pipeline.

Per the playbook, the VC begin at night.

By the time the first mortars fall, the whole place is a muddy slop sheened with whatever moonlight can cut its way through that thick overcast.

I fire the M-14 at places where the machine gun fire comes from, and hightail from one defensive position to another.

A mortar shell drops ahead, then another behind. From the sound they're the smaller 107mm shells rather than the big 120 or 160mm mothers.

I drop into one of our stations. The sandbags are already bullet-pocked, frayed edges of burlap pucker and trail fibers. Wet sand is better cover, I think as the rain fades to a drizzle.

"They're coming from there," Dinh Lu yells and points to the field of tall razor grass east of camp.

Dinh Lu has an old Browning Automatic balanced on the bags. His uniform is covered in mud. It clings to him in clumps and makes a base over his face that runs with lines of sweat and rain that glisten like spiderwebs over his cheekbones. He smells like too many cigarettes.

"Good," I say.

Both the grass and the claymores we laid in those fields should slow the VC down.

"Be advised to hold this position."

He yes-yesses me, and I'm running again.

Tracers. Explosions. Debris. Right and left. In front of me. Behind me. The smell of oil and thatch burning through the rain. C4. The ground shaking like the end of the world is here.

As always, this is when I realized I was dreaming. And, like always, knowing made everything worse. I watched myself run, feeling every step in my ankles and my knees. Pounding drove through my spine, and acid air burned my lungs. I was aware of my heart thundering inside my chest, aware of the sound of bombs bursting in the distance, and also aware that nothing I could do now would keep the mortar from falling on Dinh Lu's station, just like nothing I can ever do will stop anything else that happened that night.

Head down, both hands on the M-14, I raced to the control point, a thatched hut raised on stilts made of tree trunks. Even in the dark I see the hut's shot all to hell.

Kendrick was kneeling, pressed up against one of those trunks. He looked at me through the rain.

We had trained together three years, Kendrick and I. He was from Saginaw, and had one of the worst poker faces in the 5th. He had a girl at home and was going to be an electrician when he got back to her.

His eyes were wide and open.

He screamed, "Be advised of VC down and eastward," and he waved his hand to the same patch of high grass Dinh Lu had.

The blast hit behind him.

The image froze like it always does: Kendrick lifted up in the air, his body silhouetted in orange fire, arms and legs cartwheeling like he's some kind of cartoon.

Then came the concussion, the wave of heat, the blistering pain that burned down my leg. Everything went hazy then. There was only rain and mud and gray images of movement happening around me. Eventually I heard voices, and then the chop of the H-34 that came to get me out.

The dream stayed with me that day, like it did every day.

I was sitting in the basement of Kosmo's, a tavern on Chicago's South Side, not far from Bronzeville and not far from the lake. Special Agent Roy Mitchell was to my right, facing the door. It was June of 1969, just past noon.

Kosmo's is a dark place, a dive, really, owned by a Polish man and run mostly by his kid. It smelled like beer, cigarettes, and the burgers they would sometimes fry up in the back. A radio sat on the far end of the bar playing a tinny version of *Get Back* with Billy Preston on the keyboard.

Mitchell and I both had gin and tonics sweating into green napkins in front of us.

"Cigarette?" I said, waving a box of Winstons at Mitchell.

"No thanks."

I lit one while we waited.

As far as I was concerned, Special Agent Roy Mitchell was a star. He'd been in the bureau for more than a decade. Did a stint in Korea before that. Like me, he was an Indiana boy growing up, but he worked in Mississippi before coming here to Chicago. So, yeah, he'd been around. The guy had a way about him, too. Quiet. Mostly calm. He thought a lot more than he talked, which was more than I could say for a lot of guys who'd trained me before.

I looked at my watch. "He's late."

"He'll be here," Mitchell said.

Right on cue, the black man appeared. He was tall and thin, a little awkward in the way gangly men can be. His cheeks were hollow, his eyes slitted but busy. A mustache covered his upper lip, and he walked with that certain air about him I had seen a million times—confident, tough, but paranoid all at once.

This was William O'Neal, Chief of Security of the Chicago chapter of the Black Panthers. I couldn't help but feel edgy at the idea of it. The Panthers were an openly militant, openly communist organization, and I'd recently spent a lot of time getting shot at by openly militant communists.

He sat to my left, across from Mitchell.

Mitchell waved at the bartender and a tall glass of soda, complete with a straw, appeared a moment later.

O'Neal read my expression. "Everything goes better with Coke, right, brother?" He picked up the glass and drank. When he put it down, I felt rebuked.

"How are you, William?" Mitchell said.

"I'm good, Roy," William replied. "Who's the boy?"

"Meet Detective Radner," Mitchell said, waving an open-palmed hand my way.

"He okay?"

Mitchell smiled and gave me a crosswise glance. "Greenhorn, but he's got promise."

William gave me the once-over. I picked up the box of smokes and offered him one. He took it, but didn't light up.

"What do you have for me?" Mitchell said, sipping his drink again.

"Lots of talk about Bobby."

"I suppose that would be," Mitchell replied.

Bobby was Bobby Seale, who was awaiting trial for his part in the riots at the Democratic National Convention last summer. Both he and Huey Newton, the original founders of the Panthers, were now behind bars, a fact that, combined with Eldridge Cleaver having run off to Algeria, wasn't helping the group any.

"We got maybe three hundred across town now."

"Members?" Mitchell clarified.

"Yeah. Three hundred brothers and sisters."

"Weapons?"

O'Neal proceeded to list off guns and ammunition stored in several places around town, but focused on Panther Headquarters. His tone of voice was controlled, his statements were made in a straightforward manner, like he was reading off a menu. There was no ideology there. No sense of concern and no clandestine whispering. Just recitation. Just the facts.

"They're all legal, though," O'Neal said at the end.

The twitch of Mitchell's lips said he didn't care for that part of the answer, but O'Neal just shrugged.

"New people?"

"No one big."

"Bobby Rush? Freddie Hampton?"

"Still here." O'Neal sipped his soda. "Deborah's still pregnant."

Mitchell looked at me. "That's Hampton's girlfriend."

I nodded. Given Hoover's total hard-on for the Panthers, the BBP org chart was among the first things I learned as I came up to speed with Chicago's inner workings. Bobby Rush was now minister of defense. Fred Hampton was the chairman of the Illinois chapter. Deborah Johnson was, as Mitchell said, Hampton's girlfriend. She was carrying their child.

O'Neal spent a few minutes discussing the training of new members—the Panthers took their ideology seriously, and constant discussion was part of their program. He described the

Panther's work on the street: meetings with the Blackstone Rangers, operations for their free breakfast program, and conversations Panther officers held about how to work with the Weathermen, the Young Lords, and several other radical left-wing groups.

"That's a lot of people," I said.

O'Neal gave me a doleful stare. "Chairman Fred's not afraid to work with anyone."

He finished off the soda.

"Anything else?" Mitchell said.

"Not I can think of."

Mitchell reached into his breast pocket with two fingers and removed an envelope. He placed it on the table, and slid it toward the black man.

O'Neal folded it over once, then put it in his pocket.

"Meet again in two weeks?" Mitchell said.

"Wouldn't miss it for the world," O'Neal replied as he stood up. "Nice to meet you, detective," he said to me.

Then he left.

"What did you think?" Mitchell asked as he chewed a handful of peanuts.

"I'm surprised you paid him."

"Why?"

"He didn't give us anything on the Bradford case."

The detective finished his drink, then placed it on the table.

"We weren't here for the Bradford case."

I squinted at him and stubbed out my cigarette. I had already learned how to keep my mouth shut when I wasn't connecting all the dots yet, so I didn't say anything about the murder I thought we were investigating.

"And the other stuff?"

"What about it?"

"We already know everything he said."

"Yes, we do."

"So how was that worth $300?"

"You're Green Beret," Mitchel said, his eyes taking on a sparkle that felt oddly personal. "I would've figured you to be quicker on the uptake."

I stayed quiet.

Mitchell looked me square in eye. "Here's the deal, Carl. Chicago's no different from the jungles, all right? Sure, the streets might look civilized as shit to the average Joe, but that's a fake draw. This is a hard town, you hear me? Cops, gangs, crazy-assed hippies zoned on acid…it's a war zone out here. I know you saw your share of war zones, and you know I've seen mine. So you can trust me that I ain't shitting you on this. This city's full assholes like the Panthers. Guys who got no problem putting a .45 upside your head any day of the week. So you keep your eye on the ball, right? You keep all your cards in the game because you never know when you're going to need something special."

"You're calibrating him," I said, understanding. "He's corroborated what we know."

Mitchell's smile told me I was right.

"It's worth a few hundred bucks every now and again to know young William tells the truth, don't ya think?"

Something in his eye told me that, yes, that was what I thought.

I got home late that night.

I was tired, and my leg hurt. My brain was on overload with how much I had to learn about the job: picking up caseload on the fly, making connections within the office, learning how to deal with CPD. The assignment with Mitchell had been a huge boost to my ego, but the extra field work took so much time that by the end of the day I just wound up feeling deeper and deeper in the same hole I had been in when I first got to the office in the morning.

Had I screwed the pooch going civilian?

Maybe.

There was more going on tonight than pure fatigue, though.

I might be able to hide these kinds of things from everyone else, but I learned a long time ago not to pretend to myself.

"You all right?" Marjorie said as she put a beer and a plate heaped with meatloaf and potatoes in front of me. The smell alone made me realize how long it had been since lunch.

"I'm fine."

Our little TV was on the kitchen counter and had been turned to face her while she was cooking. She reached over, scooted it around, and sat down to her own plate. *My Three Sons* was on. It wasn't her favorite, but it was Thursday, so *Bewitched* would be next. She loved *Bewitched*. Neither of them were any *Bonanza* as far as I was concerned, and definitely not *Gunsmoke* or *Get Smart*.

"You don't look fine," she said. "Your leg acting up?"

"No, babe, I'm fine."

"Did the White Sox lose again?"

"I said I'm fine, honey."

She sat back with a sharp movement, and her face got clouded enough that even an idiot like me could see she was upset.

"I'm sorry," I said.

"I'm just trying to help."

"I know you are. I'm sorry."

Marjorie was one of the special kinds of women. She married me just before I shipped out, and dealt with all the things a woman deals with when her husband is off in the jungle. When I came back and told her I wanted to finish Bureau training, she was right there with me again. Now she was working at a legal office during the day, filing papers and getting coffee or whatever the hell else they do in a legal office. Then she came home and made dinner.

She deserved something more than I was giving her, but what was I supposed to say? *I met a Black Panther today, honey. Great guy. We should have him over for dinner sometime.*

Of course not.

First, I didn't know what to think about the Black Panthers to begin with. On one hand, this is America and I took a crap load of shrapnel to ensure that every American gets to say whatever the hell they want to say. On the other hand, I work in an organization that's about control. Control is peace. Militant radicals are, by definition, hard to deal with.

Second, there are some kinds of secrets you don't tell anyone, not even your spouse—especially not your spouse.

And, third, this was a helluva dangerous secret, really.

The meeting with William O'Neal gnawed at my gut all afternoon. I had walked into Kosmo's thinking O'Neal was going to be a garden-variety snitch, a guy who sold some stiff down the river to help us figure out the deal on Jonet Bradford's murder, a case we thought had ties to organized crime in New York and Philadelphia. I knew we were going to pay him, and I figured that money would flow right into some Panther program—which made me angsty in a totally different way. But that's not what was going down here. William O'Neal was, purely and simply, an undercover agent working for the FBI, a man who had infiltrated the Black Panthers, a spy who walked into the cold.

I knew spooks back in Vietnam, of course.

In certain situations good intel can be life and death.

But the FBI was in the law enforcement profession, not the spy business. We were supposed to be Melvin Purvis and Elliot Ness, not Boris and Natasha.

I was never any great lover of the Panthers, of course. They made me nervous as hell and caused no end of trouble. Clearly it was helpful to know what they were doing, and clearly it was easy to argue that spying on the Black Panthers could help us keep people safe.

Still.

This was America.

The thing that gnawed at me most was the way Mitchell went about the whole thing—as if running an agent to dig up crap on citizens in country was just something you did every day. I had heard of this kind of thing before. It was why I went to Vietnam. I didn't mind the idea of the Black Panthers disappearing, of course. Not at all. But the idea of the FBI doing the removing made me feel like I'd eaten something that had gone off.

On the other hand, I'd been in the jungle myself.

I'd done a lot of things I wasn't particularly proud of.

I took a bite of my dinner. The meatloaf was perfect.

"How was your day?" I asked.

Marjorie's face lightened up and she launched into a conversation about Lorraine, the paralegal at the office, and about John, who was an up-and-coming lawyer who everyone said was probably going to be a partner soon.

I drank the beer, and ate the meatloaf.

I told her about the training sessions I was scheduled for and I told her I would give her a rundown about my cases when it was proper.

All the while I hoped it would actually become proper sometime soon, because while I'm used to dealing with security and shit that's classified it was getting to be uncomfortable as hell to be doing a job that you just can't talk about at all.

By the time we finished dinner and cleaned up, *Bewitched* was on.

We settled into the couch to watch it.

I was asleep before Elizabeth Montgomery twitched her nose.

The next time I saw William O'Neal was late July.

The Cubs were playing later that day and I was going to sneak out and do the businessman's special. They were on top of the Eastern Division—the first time there ever was such a thing. Five games better than New York, a bunch more over the Cardinals. I'm more of a football guy, but a winner is a winner.

Larry Roberson, a Panther brother, had been shot down by a cop a week earlier.

"What do they expect?" Mitchell said to O'Neal after O'Neal described the anger that was flowing through the black community. "They shot officers. You can't expect the police to take it easy when you bring out the guns."

"That goes both ways."

"Cops say the Panthers shot first."

"That's not how it went down," O'Neal said, his jaw actually clenched. "And you know it."

"Our reports are corroborated by witnesses."

O'Neal sat back, then finally shrugged and ate a beer nut, then pulled on his drink. "You're the one asking what's going down," he finally said. "I'm just saying what the brothers're saying."

He glanced at me with an expression that had a sense of distance to it. It felt like everything was disconnected, like William O'Neal knew he was living in a different place than the rest of us and there wasn't anything he could do to change it. All of a sudden it felt like I was sitting in some extra dimension of the *Twilight Zone*, floating away out in space.

"Why are you doing this?" I asked O'Neal.

"Doing what?"

The expression on Mitchell's face said he wasn't going to stop me in front of O'Neal, but that he wished with every fiber of his body that I would keep my goddamned mouth shut.

I wanted my world to make sense, though. I like facts, and I like facts that line up. That's why I came to the bureau to begin with. O'Neal's reports were certainly "facts" in their own way. But the expression his face came from a deeper place than the dry-bones voice he used to give us the basics. "Ain't like a witness ever lied," that gaze said. "Ain't like a pig ever stretched the truth."

He never said it straight out, though.

Just left it there like a grenade in a trench, time ticking until whenever it might explode.

So what was real?

Either Larry Roberson had attacked the cops or he had died defending himself. There wasn't anything here that said which was which except for the words of people, and maybe the feelings other people had for those words. The Panthers had their truth. The cop's report told something different.

Does it matter which one is true? I thought.

In the end, does it really matter which event actually happened, or does it only matter that a man was dead who shouldn't have been dead and that two others were shot that didn't have to have been shot?

I looked at O'Neal, and I looked at Mitchell.

Doing what? O'Neal had asked.

"Nothing," I finally said. "Never mind me."

"When did William turn?" I asked Mitchell after the envelope was transferred and O'Neal was gone. "How did you make it happen?"

Mitchell looked at his Timex and determined we had a little time.

"Classic case, I suppose," he replied. "William and a buddy stole a car and got caught crossing state lines."

"Making it a federal thing," I said, trying to prove my chops. I drank the last of the gin and tonic, tasting the sour lime and cracking part of a rounded ice cube in my back teeth while Mitchell finished.

"Yeah. I called him up and offered him a deal. Offered to drop him a steady stream of envelopes if he would join the Panthers and tell me all about it."

"Simple as that?"

"William likes his bread buttered as much as the next guy, I suppose. But, then, I guess we all do, right?"

"Yeah," I said. "I guess we do."

On November the 9th, the Bears beat the Steelers 38-7. Bobby Douglass threw for two touchdowns. Gayle Sayers ran for 112 yards and added a pair of scores. Dick Butkus kicked ass because Dick Butkus always kicked ass. It raised the Bears' record to a stunning one victory over eight losses.

I missed the game itself, but read about it in the *Tribune* the next afternoon.

The news about Butkus made me grin.

Before Marjorie and I came here, Dick Butkus was my image of Chicago. Tough. Mean. Territorial and borderline animalistic, but brilliant at the most important defensive position on the field. My favorite story about Butkus was that one time he called time out with ten seconds to go in the game merely so he could hit someone again. To me, Dick Butkus in his black "51" was

Chicago, and Chicago was Dick Butkus. Nothing I had seen since we got here served to say any different.

Thumbing the pages, I saw another story, too.

By the end of the month, the US military said the toll in Vietnam would crest 300,000 casualties, 40,000 dead.

I rubbed my leg as I sat at my desk.

The image of Dinh Lu came to me.

I looked at the headline and thought about the number: forty thousand.

It didn't include the South Vietnamese, of course. Guys like Dinh Lu wouldn't show up in that count because it would never cross the minds of the people who made the report to consider them as part of the cost of the war.

Not that I was any better, really. Until we got over there I didn't think any different. I did now, though, and the number in the paper made me mad in ways I couldn't fully say.

I believed in those guys. They deserved to be there.

I remembered the group of idiot Army who came through A Shau camp thinking they were shit. They always talked big, and said the South Vietnamese irregulars couldn't cut it, when in reality it was the regular Army who wound up breaking under the heat, the mosquitos, and the incessant tactics of an enemy they couldn't see or understand. The Green Beret understood, though.

We learned early that you had to be one with someone before they let you lead them. You had to sit with them. Eat with them. Share stories about their kids and about the lessons they had learned about how the VC operated in the field.

The handful of us had made it work.

A glance out the office window showed overcast and wind.

My knee ached more when it got like this.

Kids were protesting the war, and others like Abby Hoffman and Bobby Seale were in prison for a more radical version of the same. Martin Luther King, Jr. had been shot a year and a half ago, Bobby Kennedy a few months later. What was it for? Was it worth it?

I flashed on the expression that had covered William O'Neal's face when I asked him what he was doing. I saw the man now. At least I felt like I understood him better.

O'Neal was a man in limbo. He wasn't really a turncoat, not in so many words, anyway. Not even a hired hand, just out doing what he was paid to do. At the end of the question, William O'Neal was a man caught in the flow of a machine he didn't understand. He didn't owe the Black Panthers anything, and he didn't owe the nation anything, either. Roy Mitchell had offered O'Neal his freedom in return for information, but when the deal was struck both O'Neal's freedom and any chance at the actual justice society was owed for William O'Neal's crime of stealing a vehicle went away, just disappeared into the ether like it had never existed.

How did it come that Roy Mitchell had O'Neal's freedom to bargain with anyway?

Does freedom belong to the president?

Does it come from a judge? Is it paid for by J. Edgar Hoover?

Is war simply government asking you to fight for something they stole away in the first place?

Is justice merely a piece of property, free to be bargained and sold?

What did I get in return for the pain in my leg that I didn't have before I went to Vietnam?

I wondered about William O'Neal.

How did he rationalize what he was doing to the Panthers? When he was alone at night and all by himself, how did he feel about the fact that he was giving away their secrets?

It was a long trip home that night.

Marjorie rubbed my leg while we watched Carol Burnett.

I told you she was special.

Like any other office in the country, Chicago's FBI building feels different on a Friday. Everything is lighter because everyone's looking forward to the weekend. As I stepped into the office that morning, shaking snow off my shoes and pulling my dark toboggan cap off my head, all that was on my mind was that Marjorie and I were going to see a movie later.

I realized something was happening as I slipped my coat off.

The room was tense. Everything felt like it was sitting on edge.

"What's wrong?" I said.

"Guess you didn't see the paper," Mitchell replied.

The *Tribune* was open on his desk beside the initial police report. The headline was circled in red pencil.

No Quarter for Wild Beasts.

Several more cops had been shot by Black Panthers, two dead. I picked it up and scanned the story. It described an ambush and explained how the cops had been attacked with shotgun blasts from positions in an abandoned hotel on the South Side.

"Washington Park," I muttered as I read.

One Panther was dead, another shot and charged with murder.

The headline was a clear call for harsh and immediate justice, and the final paragraphs of the report made it clear that Panthers were armed degenerates who had now forfeited any expectation of due process.

This had gotten personal.

Deeply personal.

"Get your coat on," Mitchell said, his voice as strained as the rest of the room felt. "We're going to get something to eat."

We met at a place called the Golden Torch this time.

It was downtown. More formal than Kosmo's, though just as dimly lit. They had cloth over the tables and actual menus. Given the weather and the time of morning, it's no surprise we were the only ones in the joint.

Mitchell and I sat waiting with just coffee cooling in front of us. A notepad sat at the edge of the table—one of those thin folders bound in black plastic that came from the supply cabinet. The pad of paper was thin and white.

"You ever wonder why we're doing this?" I asked.

Mitchell pressed his lips together, then shook his head. "I know why *I* do it," he said. "How about you?"

I was going to answer him when I saw William O'Neal arrive. He came and took his traditional seat across from Mitchell.

"I need updates," Mitchell said, not offering coffee.

William nodded. He looked tired. "You know the story's different than they put in the papers, right? Brothers didn't shoot first."

"Where is Fred Hampton?"

"Wasn't him."

"That's not the question I asked, William." The detective's voice was calm and controlled, but it didn't take any special analysis to feel the difference in his demeanor.

"He's in California. Vacationing."

All three of us knew Black Panthers didn't vacation in California. Black Panthers go to California to meet up with other Black Panthers and discuss national issues. Los Angeles, Denver, New York, Chicago. The Panthers ran as intricate an organization as we did. We also heard rumors that the organization was planning to move Hampton up to take open positions they needed to fill due to the absence of Cleaver, Newton, and Seale. David Hilliard, their current National Chairman, was struggling with the law, too, so a trip to LA could mean a lot of things, none of them very vacationy.

"I'll give you one more chance," Mitchell said, grinding his jaw. "Where does Hampton live?"

"He and his girl got a place up on Monroe."

"West Side?"

"Any other Monroe you know?"

"Tell me about the guns."

"They got 'em there. But they're all legal."

Mitchell stared ice.

"I want types, William. I want calibers and models. I want serial numbers. I want to know what kind of ammunition they have, and how many people they got staying there, you got it?"

The agent flipped open the notepad, and pulled out a pen. He put the pen beside the page, and turned it around to make it easy for O'Neal to handle.

"Draw me a map, William. I figure you've been there. I want a map of the floorplan. I want details."

A chill ran up my spine, and I could tell William and I came to the same conclusion at the same time.

William drew a breath, then picked up the pen.

He rolled it between his fingers, and began to draw.

Mitchell drove us back to the office.

The roads were clear, but still slick in places. A dusting of snow swirled in the wind, and clouds of vapor came from manhole covers at each intersection. The vinyl seats creaked against the fabric of our overcoats. The screech of old wiper blades rocked back and forth every time he toggled them on and off.

"I don't know if I can do this," I said.

He stared over one shoulder as he guided the car, the question unasked.

"You're going to give the cops that map, aren't you?" I said.

"That's the game, Carl. You understand that, right? They took two of ours, we take at least two of theirs."

"Hampton didn't do it."

Mitchell grimaced. He knew I was right. He understood completely the truth they were getting ready to embark on was one the cops and the FBI were going to create.

"You think that's important?"

"Of course it is."

"No, it isn't." He shook his head. "This is a war, Carl. Remember that. We're fighting a war here, and the Panthers are the enemy. If you don't get that, then maybe you're not the man I thought you were."

I sat in silence.

"Besides," Mitchell added. "Who's to say Hampton didn't order those killings? This is the Panthers we're talking about."

"If we can prove it he goes down."

"When they go hunting cops, the rules change."

"He's got a kid on the way."

Mitchell didn't say anything.

I watched the sidewalk roll past until we came to the office. He checked in through security and found a spot in the enclosed lot.

"I don't know, Roy. I don't think I can do this."

"I'm a good judge of character, Carl. I'm pretty sure you can."

"Let's try it another way," I argued. "Let's put everything we've got on proving Hampton ordered it. Or let's get William on it. You know he can find things if we give him some time. If Hampton made the call, he goes down."

Mitchell turned the car off, then sighed as we sat in silence.

He looked old in the light of the garage. The lines of his face were black slashes down his cheeks. His hair, cut regulation short, could still pass in the service but was shot with streaks of silvery gray that gleamed in the winter light. Folds of skin around his eyes grew soft, almost fatherly.

"Check the glovebox," he said, raising an eyebrow.

I hesitated, then punched the button that released the box.

It fell open with a clunk, and there, on top of old maps and registration cards, on top of a tire gauge and a pair of honest-to-goodness gloves, was a thin manila envelope that bulged a bit in the middle.

I pulled it out, looked at Mitchell one more time, and opened it.

Inside were pictures.

Me and a girl that had happened when I was on furlough in Saigon.

My throat got dry.

It had been a stupid night. I was tired, and I was drunk. So drunk.

Heat rose to my cheeks and the tips of my fingers actually felt like they were burning where they touched the photos.

"I think you can do this, Carl."

Marjorie lit a cigarette and blew the smoke away while I ate the last of my pork chop. She was wearing a red turtleneck and had gussied up her makeup for date night. We were at a place on East Division Street, sitting next to the glass window where the chill of the night leaked in to put up a fight with the sharp sense of embarrassment I felt every time I looked at her.

No. That was a lie.

If I was going to get anywhere with this, I had to face it straight up. I loved my wife. A little bit of Chicago bitterness couldn't stand up against the pain of knowing what a dumbass I had been. Every time I looked at her I felt the sensation of the photos against my fingertips. Every time she smiled I got a shadowed image of the woman in them.

"Let's see *Easy Rider,* instead," Marjorie said.

"I thought you wanted to see that other thing with Burt Lancaster."

"And Deborah Kerr?"

"Yeah. That one."

"I do." She looked at me from across the table as the waitress brought our check. The girls in the office had apparently been going cuckoo over Burt Lancaster and Deborah Kerr getting together again for the first time since *From Here to Eternity*. It was all she had talked about for a week.

"So, what gives?" I said. "One of the girls say old man Lancaster keeps his shirt on?"

"You wish."

I looked at the check and pulled money out of my wallet.

Marjorie smoked. "I just thought you might like to see something more like *Easy Rider.* Everyone says it's good, too. Like someone might get an Oscar out of it or something."

"Can't beat that, I suppose."

"Besides," she said, giving me one of her more dangerous looking smiles. "The Esquire is closer, and *Easy Rider* starts at eight, so maybe we'll get home a little earlier."

I raised an eyebrow.

"Well," she said, crossing her arms over her chest. "You don't have work tomorrow."

"That's true enough." Thank God.

Seeing me put my wallet away, she handed the smoldering cigarette across the table like she always did. I took it and smoked while I pulled my hat from the rung I hung it on earlier.

"I'm thinking of quitting," she said.

"Again?" I replied as I blew smoke toward the ceiling. There was something to her voice that made me stop though. "You mean your job, don't you?"

She smiled again and I understood where she was going.

"You're back for good, right, Carl? No more Army. And you've got a great job now. Steady."

I nodded. "Yeah, that's right."

She leaned in.

"Do you think it's time, yet?"

"You mean for a kid, right?" I said, probably too fast.

"I mean for a family."

I hesitated, this time probably for too long. "I don't know. I...I just...I haven't thought about it, I guess."

"Just like a guy."

That was the thing about Marjorie. She was good about this kind of thing. She knew how to bring issues up in an easy way, but was just as hard to figure out. I couldn't, for example, tell if she was hurt by this response or if she had been expecting it and was merely letting me have space to sort it out.

"Well," she said, "think about it, all right?"

"Yeah. All right."

"In the meantime, *Easy Rider*?"

"Sure," I said.

We did the eight o'clock show.

When we got home I took Marjorie out of her red turtleneck and we made love. Later, in the darkness of our room, I laid there and listened to her sleep.

"You sit and watch," Mitchell told me before we got out of the car. "It's important you get a grip on out how this shit works if you're going to make it. You got that?"

It was a Wednesday morning. Cold as sin, but no snow, yet.

The parking garage smelled of concrete and exhaust, which made sense because that's what it looked like, too. It was the essence of Chicago, I thought. The under-girder of a no-nonsense town.

On the outside, the city's skyscrapers stood tall and rugged, built with an architecture meant for a man with a certain kind of common sense. On the surface the people of Chicago went to work despite the wind and the snow and the powers of Lake Michigan just outside their doors. It's a city of action, a place where people came not to become anything, but do something instead. Chicago was like the country's Grand Central Station, I'd decided. Walking the city could make a man feel connected to everywhere else if he wanted to be.

In practice, this means it's a place where waves of people crashed into each other. Negro, Irish, Polish, Italian, Greek, Chinese, German. Male and female. Christian, Muslim, Jew, Hindu, Buddhist. Somehow it all had to work, and on the outside it did.

The city's undercarriage, though, had its own sense of pragmatism.

Here, cause and effect were sometimes one and the same.

The Machine, political and otherwise, moved in ways that maybe no one liked or maybe they did, but in ways everyone just looked away from because to do anything else would throw a spanner into the works and bring the whole goddamned thing to a grinding, shuddering halt.

To understand this, is to strip the city down to its concrete and its exhaust.

Sitting in the car, I looked at Special Agent Roy Mitchell.

"Yeah," I said, blowing into my already gloved hands. "I got it."

The meeting was held in a small office of the Chicago Police Department's Gang Intelligence Unit, a room that reeked of cigarettes, body heat, and a familiar tang of military fervor cloaked in something that might or might not have been discipline.

The session was brief and to the point.

The men of the GIU were focused. They listened with intensity.

We gave them people. We gave them events and relationships. We gave them what O'Neal told us about weapons, though Mitchell redacted mention of whether they were legal or not. And, of course, we gave them the map, which O'Neal had conveniently marked to show where Hampton's bed was.

We gave them a date, too: The date when Fred Hampton would be back from LA, and when William O'Neal would be visiting—a date when O'Neal might well find himself able to drop a mickey into a drink or two.

Through it all, I sat in a padded seat with a squeaky wheel that was stuck in one position and watched the conversation go down, thinking about Marjorie and thinking about that night, that one stupid night when the CIA photographed me doing something I had never done before and had never done again. Could they have arranged it? Was it possible I had fallen into a Hoover ploy? A stereotypical FBI joke? Gin up dirt on everyone just in case it becomes useful someday later?

Roy Mitchell had been my hero since I met him, and fact was he was a good agent—good at his job, anyway. Did he have some kind of skeleton in his own closet that his superior was pulling on him, or was he doing this on his own dime because he thought this was how it should all work? What was the truth? Did it matter?

I sat there thinking about the Panthers, and about the team of cops who were going to visit an apartment on the West Side of Chicago at 4 AM. I thought about Dinh Lu, and forty thousand. I thought about the expression on Joe Kendrick's face, frozen in time.

"Can you get the warrant?" Mitchell asked at the end.

"With the kind of firepower you say they got, I could get a warrant against my grandmother," one of the GIU men replied.

"Your grandmother a Panther?" another added.

"Nah," he said. "My granny may well want to shoot my ass, but she ain't dark enough to be a Panther."

Everyone laughed.

It was just over a week later. December 4th.

The office was buzzing by the time I got in. I didn't need to read the initial ops reports to know the details, but I did anyway.

The shootout had lasted ten or fifteen minutes, tops.

Nine Panthers had been in the apartment. Four were wounded.

The two dead were Chairman Fred Hampton and Mark Clark, a Panther visiting from downstate Peoria who had been shot through the heart. They were taken to the Cook County morgue.

The other seven were arrested and charged with attempted murder, aggravated battery, and armed violence. The wounded were taken to Cook County Hospital, the rest to the Cook County jail.

Later that night, I found William O'Neal to get more details.

"Chairman Fred wasn't dead at first," he told me.

So he was executed. Two shots to the head from close range.

That was the Panther truth, anyway.

The Cook County State's Attorney had another story.

"While serving a warrant to search for illegal weapons, our brave officers staved off a vicious attack by the Black Panthers," the statement said. "It was a miracle that none of our men was killed."

The next morning I rose early because I wasn't sleeping anyway. I was out of the apartment before Marjorie woke up. Now I was standing on an open street in the December cold. The smell here was bitter. Dead blades of wet brown grass clung to cracks in the sidewalk below my feet.

"What are you doin' here?"

The question came from a black woman standing at the end of the line when I joined.

It was a question I had asked myself a hundred times since I finished breakfast and came to my final decision. For whatever reason, hubris or simple ignorance, the police had left the apartment scene open. O'Neal told me the Panthers were giving public tours. Said people were lining up to see it.

What are you doing here?

The woman's voice sounded flat when she challenged me.

Her eyes were sharp and questioning.

She held her overcoat closed hard against her chest. She'd wrapped a blue and white scarf tight around her head. Her dress was long under the overcoat and had some kind of print to it, but her ankles were bare to the elements. Her shoes were snub-nosed and worn.

She shivered in the cold.

What are you doing here?

"I had to see for myself," I said.

For a moment it looked like she was going to say something else, but then her lips pursed together and a sense of resolution came over her face. She turned her back to me and pulled the coat tighter.

It was a long line. A single-file of people that snaked down Monroe Street like a line to a circus freak show, which I suppose it was. The front of the line ended at the doorway to 2773, where less than thirty-six hours ago Fred Hampton and Mark Clark had lost their lives.

Our conversation drew stares, though, and I realized that until then the line itself had been silent. The only sounds were wind and cold, the occasional cough and the shuffling of feet. A man several steps ahead lit a pipe, the lighter throwing a full flint click. A car drove by.

Otherwise, nobody said a word.

These were Fred Hampton's people come to see the truth, come to stand here in this silence that was covered now in a kind of electric tension that built itself up slowly up as we stood in the icy cold.

They examined me, though. I felt it when they turned to me, their eyes sometimes guarded, sometimes defiant. I felt it in the color of my skin, which was too white now. I felt it in my hair, which was still cut Green Beret short, and I felt it in my shoulders that now were covered in an overcoat that screamed FBI better than any badge ever could. I felt it when Negroes took positions behind me.

Pig. That's what I heard, and that's what I felt.

The line stepped forward and I followed the woman.

The line was long enough it took over an hour to get in.

Later, I would learn Fred Hampton played football in high school and that his father worked for years at a corn plant. Over time I would come to see his ability to connect to people and his drive to serve the community he came from. When I did I would understand exactly why Hoover and the bureau had targeted him. I would hear the core of what Fred Hampton was saying, and this line of people and this feeling of tension that ran through it would all make sense. But until then all I knew was that there were a lot of people here and that it was cold as hell, but that there was no way I would leave until I saw the inside of this apartment.

Then, suddenly, I was there.

"Don't touch nothing, don't move nothing," a Panther said as my footsteps clomped up the wooden stairway. "We want to keep everything just the way they is."

I pressed my hands into my coat pockets and stepped through the entryway and into the bullet-blasted living area.

Words cannot describe it.

Pools of blood and spattered plasterboard walls shot to shards. Broken glass. Tables overturned. Tattered posters flapping free. Record albums strewn across the floor. "Here's where brother Mark was killed," a man said, pointing to a dried red-brown pool. I stepped to the hallway, past one bedroom to the next. An armchair was ripped to shreds. A dresser drawer sat open and unhinged.

"Here's where they blew Chairman Fred's brains out," the guide said.

It was a tiny bedroom, maybe ten-by-ten.

The mattress was soaked in dried blood.

Soaked like the floor where Fred Hampton had been dragged away.

A chair and a reading lamp stood nearby, giving the whole thing a surreal sense of normalcy that pulled my brain into pieces.

Who are you?

What are you doing here?

I was struck by how small the place was. No more than forty feet front to back. Six rooms, including the kitchen out back, paperboard walls strafed to Swiss cheese by bullets.

There had been what, nine Panthers and fourteen policemen here?

I pressed my hands harder into my pockets, but leaned in to scan the bullet holes.

Sixty of them? Eighty? My eyes moved across the scene with a practiced ease. No. A hundred. Maybe more. A hundred bullets: Every one of them coming from the direction the police came, aimed low and toward the bed.

"This was no shootout," I said, speaking for the first time since I stepped into the line.

"No shit, brother," a voice echoed.

I had known what was going to happen, but the brutality here froze my chest. The room was suddenly colder than the line outside. I thought maybe my knees would buckle.

This was Chicago, I thought.

This was America.

This was murder. Cold-blooded, politically driven murder. In other countries, we would call it an assassination.

And I had been part of it.

Suddenly I knew exactly why I was here.

It was Thursday night at ten, a week after the shooting.

Marjorie had bought new Christmas lights. They sat in a pile on our table. We were going to put them up this weekend.

In the meantime, Illinois State's Attorney Edward Hanrahan was having problems in the press. He'd released a daily string of accounts of the operation, each more belligerent than the last. Despite a significant home field advantage, it wasn't working. People were calling for investigations into the Panthers' claims that Fred Hampton was murdered.

Tonight Hanrahan's officers were going to air an exclusive show on WBBM in which they would give a mock version of the shootout to the public.

Both Marjorie and I had been following it in the *Tribune*, and I saw the daily briefings in the office. I knew exactly what story they were going to tell.

She had been talking about watching the program all through dinner, but when it came on, I knew I couldn't wait any longer.

I got up and turned the television set off.

"What are you doing?" Marjorie said.

I sank into the couch beside her, and stared out of the apartment window and into the blackness of night, wishing I had the ability to talk about things like she did.

"Are you all right?" she said.

For just a flash I thought about William O'Neal. I felt the struggle of sleeping at night beside my wife, knowing what I knew. Knowing *everything* I knew. I still didn't know how William O'Neal did it. He had even been a pall bearer at Fred Hampton's funeral. Maybe he was stronger than me. I didn't believe that, but maybe it was true. Maybe he had just given up. Maybe he didn't care. I didn't know.

But I cared. That's one thing I knew for sure.

Someday I hoped Marjorie and I would have a family together. Someday I hoped she would look me in the eye again and tell me she loved me and that she understood and that nothing had ever changed in that department.

But if I was going to be the father I wanted to be, I had to be the man I wanted to be. The man I thought maybe I had once been.

And if I was going to be that man, I had to tell her this truth.

"You're scaring me, Carl," Marjorie said. Her brow was furrowed.

"I did something a long time ago," I said, turning my gaze from the window. They were literally the hardest words I had ever said.

Her brow was furrowed. "What is it?"

"I'm sorry," I said.

Then it all came out.

Three weeks later, New Year's Eve.

The forecast was for snow.

I was back at Kosmo's, alone this time. It was late in the afternoon, nearly three. The drink was bourbon, straight. I liked the sense of fire it gave me as I drank it, liked the way it burned against my nostrils as I breathed in the smell of it.

O'Neal picked his way to the table. I had a soda already there for him.

"Where's Mitchell?"

I shrugged. "He's got other things to work on."

"I don't work for you."

"I'm not expecting you to."

The black man looked confused.

"I want you to give Bobby Rush something," I said.

Rush was the Panther's minister of defense. He had been one of Hampton's closest associates and was running the show for at least as long as it took the chapter to figure out how to move forward. The cops had raided Rush's house the day after they killed Fred Hampton, but someone tipped him off. The office pool was running about three-to-one that Rush would keep control, others said it would somehow fall to Jessie Jackson, who had come to eulogize Hampton. On the whole, the Bureau was happy about how things were falling. Most said J. Edgar had finally gotten what he wanted and that the Panthers wouldn't be able to recover, but I wasn't so sure.

"What do you have?" O'Neal said.

I put an envelope on the table.

"What's that?"

"A map of the city," I said. "Marked up to show every house the FBI knows the Panthers are using to house weapons and other equipment. There's also a listing of surveillance programs our agents are working, and a receipt he might find has an interesting set of names on it."

"Those are dangerous pieces of information if they're real."

"Tell Rush I want to help."

O'Neal laughed then. His expression said I might be more than half-crazy. "You're joking with me, right? I mean, if you think the Panthers will ever line up with a pig you are more than certifiably insane."

"I'm not a pig."

"The hell you're not."

"I know what a pig is," I said, staring him down. "I'm not it."

I dropped about half the drink down my throat, then pushed the envelope further toward him. Then I shrugged.

"Tell Bobby Rush I don't care if he burns these things or uses them to wipe his ass. Tell him I got other packages going to the papers. Tell him that I catch a Panther breaking the law, that Panther's going down. But tell him that if I see a bad agent, he's going down, too. Best as I can do it, anyway."

O'Neal looked at the envelope like it was a snake. "You know you're gonna wind up dead, right?" he said.

I finished the drink, then stood up.

"Maybe. But this is how I play it."

I dropped ten bucks on the table. "Get yourself a burger if you want," I said. "Or give it to the breakfast program. Whatever."

Outside it was cold, but not bitter. I pulled the collar of my coat up as I walked out the door to stand under the restaurant's awning. The sky was overcast, and snow was coming down in the kind of flakes you see in the movies. Big, fluffy things flying around in circles. They gave me an image of a boy in the middle of a field somewhere in Indiana, looking up and laughing as he staggered around like some kind of mummified zombie trying to catch one on his tongue.

I fished my last cigarette out of the box, then popped the top off my lighter. The flint caught and the flame rose orange and blue. The smell of burning fluid was sweet in the chilled air.

Marjorie agreed to see me at the apartment tonight. We're going to talk about what happens next.

I looked at the cigarette, still unlit, then gazed over the fresh snow.

I closed the lighter, stepped out from under the awning, and tossed the cigarette to the gutter.

As I walked into the cold, my leg felt good.

You've completed

Collins Creek, Volume 1:

Contemporary Currents

and

Historical Eddies

If you liked this collection, you might also like Volume 2 and Volume 3.

Also, if you liked this volume, it is always helpful for authors if you return to you bookseller's site and leave a review. These reviews allow other like-minded readers to find this book, and as such can help your favorite writers continue to create their work.

Thank you so much for spending your time with me!

About Ron Collins

Ron Collins is an Amazon best-selling Dark Fantasy author who writes across the spectrum of contemporary and speculative fiction.

His short fiction has received a Writers of the Future prize and a CompuServe HOMer Award. His short story "The White Game" was nominated for the Short Mystery Fiction Society's 2016 Derringer Award. He has been a contributing member to Fiction River since 2013.

With his daughter, Brigid, he also edited *Face the Strange, An Anthology of Speculative Fiction.*

He holds a degree in Mechanical Engineering, and has worked to develop avionics systems, electronics, and information technology before chucking it all to write full-time, which he now does from his home in the shadows of the Santa Catalina Mountains.

If you liked this collection, you can discover other work by Ron Collins at:

Follow Ron at:
http://www.typosphere.com
Twitter: @roncollins13

Sign up for Ron's Newsletter and get a free ebook!
http://www.typosphere.com/newsletter

Other Work by Ron Collins

Stealing the Sun (6 Books)

STARFLIGHT

STARBURST

STARFALL

STARCLASH

STARBOUND

STARCRASH

Saga of the God-Touched Mage (8 Books)

GLAMOUR OF THE GOD-TOUCHED MAGE

TRAIL OF THE TOREAN

TARGET OF THE ORDERS

GATHERING OF THE GOD-TOUCHED

PAWN OF THE PLANEWALKER

CHANGING OF THE GUARD

LORD OF THE FREEBORN

LORDS OF EXISTENCE

The PEBA Diaries (2 Books)

SEE THE PEBA ON $25 A DAY

CHASING THE SETTING SUN

Standalone Novels

Wakers

The Knight Deception

Short Story Collections

Picasso's Cat & Other Stories

Five Magics

Tomorrow in All the Worlds

Follow Ron at:

http://www.typosphere.com

Twitter: @roncollins13

Newsletter: http://typosphere.com/newsletter

Acknowledgements

I would like to thank all the authors, editors, publishers, and other people who contributed to the Oregon Coast (and Las Vegas) Anthology Workshop, without which none of these stories would exist. Special thank you to Kristine Kathryn Rusch for her very kind introduction to this volume. And, as always, thanks to my wife, Lisa, for pretty much everything.

www.ingramcontent.com/pod-product-compliance
Lightning Source LLC
Chambersburg PA
CBHW070503200726
48293CB00007B/2348